B. HORROR

B. HORROR

KCL

and other stories

Wendell Mayo

Livingston Press
at
The University of West Alabama

ISBN 0-942979-61-3, paper
ISBN 0-942979-62-1, cloth
Library of Congress Catalog Card Number: 99-64441

Manufactured in the United States of America.
Printed by Patterson Printing

Text layout and design: Jill Wallace
Cover photo: Tricia Taylor. Special thanks to Mary Pagliero and Richard Day, fo
being good sports.
Cover design: Joe Taylor
Proofreading: Stephanie Parnell, Kim Smith, Jennifer Stillion, and Joe Taylor

Acknowledgements: "Robert's Bride" previously appeared in *The Yale Review*; "B. Horro
in *The Missouri Review* (as Finalist in the National Editor's Prize Competition); "Overture
in *The Chicago Review*; "Dance of Eights" in *Alaska Quarterly Review*; "Who Made You"
West Branch (and received Special Mention in the *Pushcart Prizes Anthology, XIX*); "Ma
Magdalena Versus Godzilla" in *Confrontation*; "Mortal Sins" in *Vignette*; "Day Cook"
Fish Stories: Collective 2; "Going Long" in *The Little Magazine*; "Woman Without Arm
in *The Ledge Poetry and Fiction Magazine*; and "The California Franchise Tax Board"
Verve. Thanks to Gerrit Henry for permission to use his poetry.

The author would also like to thank MacDowell Colony, Yaddo, and The Edward F. Albe
Foundation for their generous support.

Table of Contents

I. The Watchers

II. From the Wall

Other books by the author:

Centaur of the North (Arte Público Press)
In Lithuanian Wood (White Pine Press)

For Amy, Jennifer, and Pete

I. The Watchers

Subtle, subterranean way,
The movie gives me courage,
Just by its viciousness.
It is a presence—like it
Or not—in my warm apartment.
It gives me courage
To sit down and turn
To my typewriter,
And write you, and me,
An alternative,
Write away the horror,
Write away the blood,
The inevitable, quick progression
Of another American night.

—*Gerrit Henry,*
from "The Watchers"

ROBERT'S BRIDE

The very life seems warm upon her lip.
—Polixenes, *The Winter's Tale*

Robert's older than me, but not much. His hair is dark and he still has most of it. You can smell his hair tonic, which mostly smells like alcohol. Sometimes, it's hard to differentiate how Robert's hair tonic smells from the smells in the Lacquer Room where they are priming Cutlass quarterpanels today.

Robert comes straight over to me in the break room, sits, and goes into his lunch sack with both hands. He fishes out a Slim Jim beef stick, strips the plastic off, and begins to chew on it. Robert's a well-kept guy. Thin. But I don't know how he stays thin, the way he eats. He's one of those guys who can eat everything in sight and never has to worry about getting fat. He has no concept of calories, no scruples about eating whatever he pleases. Now Robert pauses, sets the stick down, and begins to unbutton his shirt.

He spreads the lapels of his denim shirt apart.

"The Bride got me this T-shirt last night," he says proudly. The T-shirt underneath says: NEVER TRY TO TEACH A PIG TO SING; IT WASTES YOUR TIME, AND ANNOYS THE PIG.

Robert is beaming. "What do you think?" he asks me.

I am thinking about *Pygmalion* and *My Fair Lady*, trying to remember which came first. I have nothing to say, like I usually have nothing to say. But I grunt politely so Robert won't ask me again what I think.

Robert pulls out a Twinkie from his sack, eats half, and stuffs it back inside. He leans over and pushes the bag into the overstuffed trash container by the table.

"See you later," he says, and goes off to the Details Department to emboss more OLDSMOBILE insignias.

I mount twenty-four bucket seats before lunch, which is really cooking. The foreman makes a special effort to check most of the seats; he can't believe I got that many in. I go over to the lunch room about 12:15—lunch break—and pull up a chair. Robert comes over, right on time. He's rubbing his hands together: he turns them palm-up and shows them to me.

"It's that chrome paint again."

"Try some gasoline on them," I tell him.

"Jesus, I hope I can get this stuff off my hands. Tonight I'm picking up the Bride at the Beauty College. We're going over to Quiznos's for subs. You want to come?"

"I'll pass," I say; then I add, "I go out there sometimes. Maybe I'll see you."

Lately, I have found a way to protect my luncheon provisions from Robert: I bring health food most days. Robert scowls at it, and I feel weak by the end of the day, but it keeps him from getting into my lunch bag. Today, I have unflavored yogurt, rice cakes, and celery sticks stuffed with cottage cheese.

Robert reaches into his breast pocket and pulls out a chocolate bar.

"The Bride got herself a French Bun yesterday. Some of her classmates at the Beauty College gave it to her. It makes her hair look like Audrey Hepburn's in that movie *Charade*—you remember the movie?"

"I saw the flick once," I tell him, digging into the yogurt.

"One of the Bride's friends at the college did her fingernails and toenails in purple, then she plucked the Bride's eyebrows—not all of them, just the hairs that were making them look too thick. You know what I mean? Thinned them right out. Now her fellow beauticians are really going to work on her; the Bride says it'll be like a class project: *Preparing the Bride to Take Her Vows*; they'll get classroom credit; the Bride will get credit, too, since she's donating her body."

"That's a lot of free body work . . . a bargain," I say.

But it's all I can do to keep quiet. Robert's always going on about how the Bride goes to the Delta Beauty College. *College*, my ass. I went to school at the University of Detroit for three years before I quit to work at the plant. That was a real school. Delta Beauty College, what a joke. I've seen their ads on TV: *Delta can make a difference in your life*. Beauticians' College. My ever-loving ass.

Before we finish lunch, Robert tells me he doesn't want the Bride only for her body—which, he says, is sleek, firm, young, and terrific—Robert says she has a smooth personality too: *like a transmission*, he laughs. She's forward when she should be: the perfect conversationalist; she moves into dialogue with ease and precision—*class*, Robert sighs—and in reverse, the Bride is a great listener, with tact and grace; she's easily entertained—*a real human being*, Robert says. *Then of course in neutral*, he adds, *she is unobtrusive, so quiet you hardly know she's alive*.

Well, that's Robert. That's fine for a guy like him, a guy with a name like Robert. Some guys just like to get tied down, guys with names like Robert, guys who *never* ask you to call them Bob or Bobby or Bud, guys who never get called Rat's Ass or Bad Chew by other guys—even if only away from the domestic setting.

So at first I didn't know Robert at all, but the point is this: I never would have gotten to know him, except it's kind of amazing how some people, people you'd never want to get to know in a million years, in fact *especially* people you'd never want to know, just come right up and start talking. It's like the more you want to be left alone, the more they are attracted to you or something. I don't mean like *queers* or anything, I mean in a queer *way*. I mean they truly think you must want to be friends; so they wind up, inevitably, right in your face.

And that's Robert. I mean he's *okay* and everything. I mean it's easy to tell some real asshole to piss off. But Robert's not at that particular extreme. So he has coffee with me on breaks. I think it's because he doesn't have anyone else to plague with the excruciating details of his wedding plans. I'll probably never see the guy once he's married. It happens like that; it happens like that most times in good marriages. Eventually, the groom forgets his friends. But this is the countdown to the big day, so he wants to be friends, so he goes on a lot about the wedding, the Bride, his private affairs, like it is any of my business, like I really care to know.

So I told Robert I go over to Quiznos's sometimes, and I do. When I get home I have nothing to cook up, so I go get a sub—and I get it carry-out in case I run into Robert and the Bride. I leave myself the back way out: "Gee," I plan to say, "I guess I'd better get this sub home before it gets cold. . . . Nice to meet your Bride, though, Robert." Then I'll dash out. Errol Flynn. Captain Blood.

Quiznos's is one of those places with the little bell nailed to the top doorjamb. It drives me nuts when I go inside. If the place is dead, everyone gawks at you. When the place is busy, nobody notices. So I am glad it's the supper rush when I get there.

A long wood-paneled wall divides the grill from the booths. I sit at one end of the counter by the grill, and the Greek guy gets my order straight-off: the steak sub with the mushroom sauce, which really isn't anything more than hamburger and some mushroom soup concentrate from a can, but the beauty about Quiznos's is that they don't fake anything: they keep the raw burgers and soup cans in plain view. Except for the name "Steak Sub," which just kind of stuck over time, nothing in Quiznos's is done for deceptive purposes—you eat what you see: it's tradition.

I see Robert and the Bride sitting behind the paneled wall. They don't see me. Robert is talking, the Bride is not: this is typical of anyone having food with Robert.

Now you have to know this: meeting Robert and the Bride at

Quiznos's is not fate. I mean, even Robert being there is not fate, since I knew they would probably be there—so this is not consummate fate. It is more like partial fate, or chance with some fate mixed in—yet what I see is more peculiar than fate or chance: the Bride is sitting opposite Robert with her French Bun; I see her right away, at least I get a real good glimpse of the Bun towering over the paneled wall. The Bun is shaped like a beehive, and in the white light the Bun's outer edges, where the heavy razor-blue mass seems less dense, is almost stratospheric, insubstantial, soft. The muscles in the Bride's neck hold the gigantic Bun remarkably steady, like there are mysterious vectors of force underpinning the base of the Bun: to keep it from toppling. The ceiling lights in Quiznos's are harsh. The light crawls around the perimeter of the Bun in wormy rays.

I check out a few songs on the countertop juke machine. I flip through the metallic charts a couple of times. Then I get back to looking at the Bride. She has a geisha's face, and she would look like one, if not for the protracted Bun. Her skin is white and dull, like porcelain. A puzzling gauntness overcomes its roundness, which I suspect is because the rouge she wears is so red it appears to be black.

The Greek puts the sack with my sub in it on the counter, and I reach back for my wallet; and what I feel next is instantaneous, a kind of momentary freezing—I notice the Bride's eyes, mind you only her eyes under her penciled-in narrow eyebrows, move in her head and look straight at me. Dead eyes. Like glass eyes. I turn quickly to the Greek, yet the whole time I am looking at him—I pay him, take my change, and leave—I know the Bride has been looking at me with her dead eyes.

When I get home the sub is cold anyway. I put it in the microwave a minute; I start laughing. At first it feels good to laugh. I am laughing at Robert and his weird Bride. Then I realize I am alone, laughing. I mean I am alone, and laughing about Robert's Bride, and I don't feel bad or anything, just scared—I continue to laugh because I am scared— and I get more scared as time passes, laughing the way you do when you're really frightened by something, like a shadow or a noise, then the earthly reason for the apparition appears, like a cat, or a book slumping over in the library and hitting the floor—and you're relieved because it was only some object, or thing, or a cat—but you're still laughing and scared at what it might have been. Something ghastly. Something that's dead and alive at the same time. Like Robert's Bride.

The bell goes off in the microwave. I eat the sub. It is pretty good. It's good to know what's in the things you eat. Most of Quiznos's food lends itself rather well to reheating. As I eat, I am pretending Quiznos's is as classy sounding as Delmonico's. I am really hungry and still kind of freaked—and that makes the food even better.

At the ten o'clock break I ask Robert why he doesn't bid up to another job; I say he's been embossing OLDS insignias for five years. Robert says he is thinking about it; then he tries to change the subject: *Had I gotten over to Quiznos's last night?* He and the Bride are going mushroom hunting this afternoon. *Could I come along?* Robert says to try to bring a friend with me; he says it's okay to bring a *girl* but I persist with my original question: *You could get a better job here if you tried.*

Robert is making a career out of finishing his peanut butter sandwich. Finally, still chewing, he says:

"The Hindu god says it is better to do your duty badly, than to do someone else's job well."

Robert thinks this is funny. I don't know. I honestly don't know about guys like Robert. Guys who don't bother with nicknames. Guys who want to settle down. He isn't even Hindu. He's Methodist.

Robert packs his trash into his sack, crushes it into a ball and tosses it over to the can. The wad bounces on the rim and hits the floor. I tell him I'm impressed. Robert goes over, picks it up and drops it inside. He comes back and sips on his coffee for a long while. He looks around at other people, but not at me. "I wouldn't be afraid of picking mushrooms," Robert says. He keeps watching people eat, like he's really interested in it. "Getting the nonpoisonous ones mostly depends on the time of year you pick them. This is a good time to find them."

"I think I'll pass," I tell him. "Thanks anyway—as far as food goes, I'm not an advocate of individual achievement. I rely on the A&P for most foodstuffs."

That night I get home about 11:30 p.m. I have just finished a double shift at the plant. I am not hungry, but I have a beer to help me sleep. I want a sound sleep since I'll be back on my regular day shift the next morning.

I don't hear the car pull up, just the doorbell ring three times.

I go to the door and I look in the peephole. I see a woman with a thin face; the face is shocked white; the face has no makeup, and the eyebrows are plucked clean—she has no eyebrows whatsoever. The woman's platinum blonde hair folds up and lies flat across her shoulders, like fine drapery might pile itself on the floor.

The woman reaches up and rings the bell again; I back off, then I'm back at the peephole, holding my breath. The woman steps back from the door. She looks up and down the outside of my townhouse. She wears tight black leather pants and a sheer white blouse. I see she has no bra and very small breasts, shaped like acorns. She's holding a Tupperware bowl under one arm. Suddenly—in a flash—she lurches up to the peephole. I see this gigantic eye, a cold eye, a dead eye like a wet marble—then the peephole is dark.

I spring back from the door. I go back to the kitchen and finish my beer.

Later, I go back to the peephole. I see my sidewalk, the empty street. I breathe deeply several times, then I open the door. I see the Tupperware bowl on the stoop. I take the Tupperware inside and set it on the kitchen table. I have another beer before I have enough courage to open it.

Mushrooms.

Somehow I am amazed Robert shows up the next day at the nine o'clock break. I am glad he is not in intensive care, a victim of toad-stools.

Robert tells me the girls at the Beauty College are wrapping the Bride in plastic today to squeeze the cellulite from her body. He says that since there isn't much time before the wedding, the Bride thinks this is a good way to trim down. He says they got a lot of mushrooms last night, which are okay for the Bride to eat since they don't contain calories.

Robert says the Bride loves mushrooms—he says, she says mushrooms *sustain* her; *but*, he says, everyone knows there's no nutrition in them whatsoever.

Later, at the two o'clock break Robert tells me the Bride has signed-up to attend a one-week retreat sponsored by Excellence Incorporated. Robert says he is going to accompany the Bride the first day under the break-in period stipulated in the contract—he calls it the spousal visitation privilege—*did I want to come and check it out?* He tells me there is a special visitation clause in the contract for friends.

"I'll pass," I tell him, and pour coffee from my Thermos. "You want some of this?"

"Sure. You want part of my Twinkie?"

"No thanks."

"How did you like the mushrooms the Bride dropped off last night?"

"I have them in the icebox."

"They won't keep too long."

"Too bad," I tell him.

Robert goes over to the pop machine and comes back with a can of soda.

"The Bride says she needs the Excellence retreat for *professional* reasons," Roberts says, "because she wants to open a curio shop and salon after the wedding."

"That's nice."

"Yeah. . . . She wants to sell all kinds of things in the shop, but only things that are colored purple. . . . That's her angle, things that are colored purple."

"I'm not too hungry. You want my cheese crackers?"

"I think I'll pass," Robert says, and he goes back to the embossing room.

This morning, before I go to work, I'm grinding the mushrooms in the Insinkerator. It's too late to brew some coffee in the ten-cup automatic drip, so I have a quick cup of instant.

I hover over the kitchen table with the coffee cup, scanning the newspaper. I'm checking the latest quote on GMC common stock when I spot a photo and its caption: EXCELLENCE INC GRADS LOOK TO FUTURE. Robert is in the picture. He is in the back row of the graduating class with his arm around a short redheaded woman. The woman wears a gray, pin-striped ensemble. She wears wire-rimmed glasses.

It's hard to get analytical while browsing the newspaper. It's tough to get excited. Mostly I glaze over when I go through a newspaper. Many facts fly around, but only a few stick, like flies on flypaper. About the best I can do as each fact flies by is grunt approval or disapproval. So it is not until I am driving to work that it occurs to me I have observed the Bride on three occasions, and not one of these times have I seen the same woman.

I don't see Robert until lunch. He says he painted one hundred OLDS insignias this morning, a personal best. Then he goes into many details of his premarital arrangements. He tells me how the parts are coming together: they have the K of C Hall for the reception; the Bride has registered at all the stores in town for those gifts she wants most; her grandmother's gown has been resurrected for the ceremony; the cellulite squeezing is going fine; yesterday, the Bride bought a year's membership at the Peachbottom Tanning Salon. *To get some life into her skin*, Robert tells me. "Why don't you come over to my place tonight?" he adds. "The Bride and I are making spaghetti."

"I don't think so," I say, wrestling the wrapper off a sugar-free granola bar.

"Well . . . we always make extra in case you come—we eat about nine."

"I think I'll pass."

It's not that I'm in the habit of passing up a free meal. I had to weigh Robert's invitation carefully; and that meant without the intense pressure of eating in the presence of the human garbage disposal.

Later, after I got off work, I had this feeling I could set things straight about Robert and the three different women I had seen. On the other hand, could this be a single woman, one body with many skins?

When I get to Robert's townhouse, his brown VW Rabbit is parked in the street. His driveway is clear, almost like he expects me. I shut off my headlights, kill the engine and coast in behind the Rabbit. The first floor picture window is brightly lit. I can't see anyone inside. The window on the second floor has a dim, orangy light in it.

I sit in my car about half an hour, listening and waiting. It's cold out and it smells like rain. But it is not raining. Nothing changes inside the house, so I get out of my car, quietly coax the car door shut, then walk up to Robert's front door.

I knock once and Robert opens the door, pulls me in, and sits me in the La-Z-Boy by the TV.

"It'll be ready in a minute," he says out of breath, and he goes into the kitchen.

I see a colander in the kitchen, steaming, laden with noodles.

Robert runs cold water over the noodles. Then he comes back out and stands at the bottom of the stairs leading up to the bedrooms.

He shouts up the staircase: "It's soup, honey!"

Robert pauses, and turns to smile at me, to reassure me with a winsome look that he has not abandoned me—or I, him—then he races up the stairs, and comes directly down, slowly, cautiously, leading the Bride by the arm.

The Bride is wearing a long, green terry cloth bathrobe and white tube socks. The stairwell is dark, so it's nearly impossible to see her face. Robert stops at the bottom step to be sure she takes it carefully, then he brings her into the light which slants into the living room from the kitchen.

The Bride's entire head is wrapped in bandages. I get up to go, mumbling something about my headlights being on. Robert shoves me down, and escorts the Bride to the dining room table.

"The Bride has had a face lift," Robert says, pulling out a chair, helping the Bride into it and snugging her into her place at the table. "It's outpatient stuff: just a little detailing here and there. Isn't it exciting?"

Robert runs back into the kitchen, makes up two plates of spaghetti and sets them on the table. Now he takes my arm and leads me to the table. He sits me next to the Bride, who seems inanimate. She nods at me.

"Don't mind her," Robert smiles, "she doesn't feel like eating or talking. She's on a diet anyway." Robert leans close to me and says into my ear: *The Bride is just in the shop for repairs—the good news is she's still under warranty.* Then he beams: "We can't wait to see how you turn out—right, honey?"

The Bride nods at me again and Robert continues talking: "She gets the mask off Friday and we're going down to King's Island Saturday morning to celebrate."

I'm nervous. My noodles keep falling off my fork. Finally I resort to chopping them up and eating them with my spoon. Robert says: "You want to come along? We're going to ride the Beast—it's the Bride's favorite."

"I don't know, Robert," I say, trying not to stare at the bandages on the Bride's head, "I might have to cover second shift for this guy whose dad is dying."

"Maybe we'll see you there anyway," he says.

"Maybe. . . . Thanks for dinner. . . . I gotta run." I get up and make for the door. "Oh . . . nice to meet you," I say to the Bride and I close the door behind me.

She nodded at me a third time as I was leaving.

After dinner with Robert and the Bride, I drive around the block in Robert's neighborhood a few times. Each time I pass Robert's townhouse, I expect to see something: something changing, something different, maybe something awful or unbelievable. I am hoping for something.

On the fourth time around the block, I notice the lights are out in Robert's townhouse. Then the TV comes on in the upstairs bedroom. The intensity of the light in the room changes every second: shadows rise and fall along the walls like dancing snakes. I hear voices, the way you hear voices but not language, not speech. Then the Bride appears in the window, her body dark, her gauzed face luminous in the street light. She stands at the window briefly, then she moves back into the shadows. She could not have seen me. But I am sure, somehow, she has.

Sometimes it's better not to ask too many questions. Things happen, things get done and you accept them, or you must accept the things you've done, whether or not you can imagine you ever had the capability to do them in the first place. I lied to Robert about the guy whose dad was dying. I don't know why I lied; sometimes I freak and I lie; I don't even know why I freak, so how can I know why I lie?

The next day at work Robert skips the nine o'clock and the ten o'clock break. I don't see him until late in the lunch period. His eyes are red, hair disheveled and dry; his face is puffy, like he's hung over; his skin is a slight tinge of green. He comes right up to me, no sack, no snacks, no fists full of crackers or candy—he seems barren of essential sustenance.

He says: "The Bride has left me."

I say: "Why?"

He says: "I don't know, it was a silly argument over the TV. Then she started scratching at her bandages. Then she tore at them, *screaming*. Finally, she stopped everything and she ran out."

I ask him: "So where is she?"

Robert just sits there, like the bottom of the world has just dropped out, and he with it. Robert's eyes find the top of the table, then he waves his hand limply in the air: "I don't know," he says, "she's out *there*—somewhere."

I tell Robert not to worry. He doesn't hear me. Rather, he seems nervous, almost frightened instead of destitute. "I've got to get her back," he says. "She can't be out there on her own!"

I tell him I have to get back to the line. I do not consider what Robert has told me because I seldom consider anything he says with much seriousness. Then, before I can get away, Robert mentions the one thing I had not counted on.

"Do me a favor," he says as I am getting up from the table. He is nearly in tears, so I stay a moment more. Robert writes his phone number on a napkin and gives it to me. "If she comes by your place, call me—okay?"

Driving home from work, I am thinking about Robert's Bride, then I can't think about her anymore, so I am thinking about my old man. When he was trying to get me a job at the plant, my old man used to tell me, "Life is only what you do every day." I don't know. Maybe he was right. I never liked my old man. So it's hard to accept the things he told me unless I think about them objectively. *Yeah, Dad, shit happens. So what?* I prefer to think that being alive is optimism, and being dead is pessimism. Things are simple that way. When I'm down in the dumps, I look around; I look for dead things; there are always plenty of them to see—I imagine I am most alive when dead things are all around me. So when people ask me, I must say I am pretty well off—I *must* say this since it is true; it is the only option for those of us who are alive. If I could get over being so scared over small things, like mushrooms and Robert's weird Bride, things would be perfect. I might even begin to believe the things I must believe.

I stop at the A&P. They have a lot of stuff on sale, stuff like smelt, so I stock up. When I get home I water the lawn; I have a beer. After dark, I lock up. I watch all of Letterman, then Snyder. I brew ten cups of coffee in the ten-cup automatic drip; I play several games of solitaire, thinking, and laughing to myself in the crazy way I did before about Robert's Bride: *she is out there somewhere.* At Large. I make some popcorn in the microwave. I brew another ten cups. It gets really late. The whole time I didn't hear or see a thing out of the ordinary. But I could be wrong. I may have dropped off a couple of times. I don't remember. That's the only scary part. I don't remember falling asleep. I think I stayed up all night waiting for Robert's Bride to call.

B. Horror

I'm against all this petty bourgeois stuff. . . . I'm a man with
higher needs. What I'm interested in is a wardrobe with a mirror.
—Prisypkin in *The Bedbug*, Mayakovsky, 1928

I asked B. once why I always play the victim. It wasn't as if his wardrobe wouldn't fit me with a few alterations, though I'll admit, I was the one with the slender arms, white, willowy, and wonderfully understated dimple alongside my mouth when I screamed. And I practiced my scream to perfection: it began with the highest possible note a falsetto might make. Then I drove it, long and full of rumbling vibrato, until I could feel the glottis trembling in the back of my throat and the corners of my open mouth ache. I was good, like Julia Adams was good in *Creature from the Black Lagoon* . . . and why not? I was young enough, seventeen, nearly out of high school. Luckily, my voice hadn't changed. And anyone'd scream at such a hulk of black swamp rot if it were ready to foul her new wipe-on tan. Or muss his wig, falsies, and one-piece bathing suit.

B.'s answer: "You gotta scream, kid. It's the payoff. They expect it—besides," he added, "look at all the hair and muscle on me. Don't be ridiculous."

I gotta admit, he was right. B. was a little short, but he had biceps like Popeye and dark, thick hair running every which way in waves like the coat of a mongrel—his arms, back, beard—but not his head, which had a large, saucer-shaped bald spot on top, clean and shiny like a cue ball.

So I screamed and continued to scream in the employ of B. Horror Enterprises. I was the Mommy's scream in *It's Alive* when she first sees her murderous offspring. I've been every mother's scream. Name them, I've screamed at them: Giant Leeches; Brain Eaters; Living Dead; Assorted Freaks; Vampires; Werewolves; Hyde (or was it Jekyll?); Swamp Things; Chainsaws; Giant Ants, Grasshoppers, Mantises, Tarantulas, Crabs; Robot Gogs and Magogs; The Ripper; Blob, Son of Blob; and Stepford Wives (with their circuitries showing). . . .

I was the consummate, everlasting scream, holding out against the vision of everything alien, and I have screamed at the worst aberrations known to post-World War II humankind, and they just kept coming . . . coming. . . . I had my scream and B. Horror had me to make it. It was all very authentic, and working part-time I'd already played Cleveland, Evansville, Toledo, and Cincinnati, all the biggies. But eventually B. and I settled down. Our main office and venue were in Fort Wayne, Indiana, where B. promised to take me full-time into the company, so long as I continued to make my scream—and make it pay.

Not long ago, B. and I left his shop near the Memorial War Coliseum for a job at the home of Dr. Tarnower, whose daughter was making her debut, coming out, as it were. The evening air felt wonderful in Fort Wayne, a May night, so I could hear the crickets bleating, June bugs smacking against the windshield of the van, and smell the cow dung from surrounding farms. Tarnower's was in the northeast of town, just off Trier Road. He was a good customer, not that we'd ever done a job for him before, but I say "good" because he seemed to fit our demographic profile of a "good" customer. He appeared to have plenty of money and leisure time to indulge himself and his family in the sort of service we provided. And he was a linchpin of Fort Wayne, on the Council of Lutheran Churches, Board of Magnavox, all the right stuff.

So B. and I figured he'd get a kick out of what we did, as it were, along with other people like him: almost anything goes; a lot might shock them, but they don't say much about it if it does. I mean, they're folks who are simply raised to know what's right, good folks who tolerate what's wrong, wouldn't change it for the world, unless they feel something poking around in their pocketbooks. Our services were inexpensive.

So we reckoned what we did was novel enough, but not too offensive, to make Fort Wayne our headquarters and, in the case of Dr. Tarnower, that he'd reach a good sense of balance between tolerance of things alien to him and that which might offend him, because of the distance from things alien we so meticulously achieved in our performances. In fact, B. had made scrupulous observations and calculations of the distance necessary. Say you were doing a scene in which you had a monster coming at a helpless, shrieking woman. B. figured that at the start of the scene the monster should never be closer than, say, twenty feet from any one of the guests. Now, the screaming woman, I mean, in my case, the screaming woman persona, could be as close as ten feet from the guests. And B. had calculated that ten feet was the optimal distance when the creature actually assaulted the terrified woman, when both assailant and victim were closest to the customer, a kind of "critical mass" as B. used to say . . . and the monster would do whatever it was to the screaming woman he was supposed to do. But only ten feet, he warned me. No closer.

So we pulled into Tarnower's drive, one that made a kind of parabolic path, past the front door and back to the main road. The house wasn't too bad, big, but modest, a sprawling low ranch, covered on all sides with crab apple trees and dogwoods that hid the true dimensions of the house from view.

"Not bad," I said to B., looking the place over. He didn't respond, put the van in park, shut the engine off, and went to the front door. When he got to the porch, he rang the doorbell, grunted, put his hands in his pockets, and looked the place over himself. He grunted again, a grunt sounding like grudging approval, then the door opened.

"B. Horror," he said. "I'm here to set up."

He went inside the house a moment, then stuck his bald head out the frame of the door and motioned for me to come. I opened the back of the van and took out our two wardrobe cases, thinking that if B. was so blessed with testosterone, he should lug the wardrobes around for once, but I followed B. through the house with the wardrobes to a back bedroom, thinking, what's the use, he's the boss.

B. closed the bedroom door, set all our stuff on the bed, loosened the straps on the cases, broke them open, and pulled out my nightgown.

"Here," he said and smiled, holding the white gown out to me, draped over his arms, like a present. "Make yourself sexy."

I grabbed the gown from his arms and set it aside on the bed. B. took out and unfolded the plastic banner he'd prepared, one that read CREATURE FROM THE BLACK LAGOON in black, drippy lettering, like flowing, running dark blood.

"I'll be right back," he said, set the banner on the dresser, and left.

He returned from the van with a spotlight and a telescoping mounting pole, took the banner, and left again. Through the window I watched him make his way out back to Tarnower's patio and heart-shaped pool. Near a tall clump of azalea bushes opposite the wet bar, where we'd decided most guests would gather, he tied the strings at each corner of the banner to some twigs in the bushes. Next, he set up the spotlight on the mounting pole so that it would illuminate the banner and a spot on the ground directly in front of it. He took the electric cord and played it out until he found an outlet near a tool shed.

I put my slip on, then the falsies B. had made from automatic drip coffee filters, especially for the occasion. Then I slid the nightgown over my head. I took the portable vanity out of the wardrobe, set it on the dresser, made up my face, then fixed my black wig to my hair with pins. When B. came back, the guests were already moving from the house to the patio, pool, and wet bar. Tarnower, a stately man, with a white handlebar mustache, wearing a powder blue dinner jacket and white slacks, had his daughter, the deb, by the hand—a lovely girl, with a sky-blue sleeveless dress, her hair made into a small bun with a white ribbon in it that ran from the bun to the small of her bare back. She was graceful and obviously close to her father, whom she stayed very near the whole time, the way daughters did, I supposed.

I had to pee, so I checked the hallway and tiptoed down to the bathroom I'd noticed on our way in. When I passed the door before the bathroom, it was slightly ajar, and I heard voices, a woman's and a man's. . . . I'm not a nosy person. I'll go a long way around a scuffle, and I'm not proud of that either, though I'm not sure why confrontation scares me; but bad timing, it seemed to me, was not the better part of valor—and I could not help hear him hit her and her body thunk against the inside wall, followed by a kind of metallic clang.

I heard her say, "I'm going to scream."

I heard him say, "I don't care. . . . Go ahead. I can take it or leave it."

He hit her again, and I guess it was her elbows I heard knock against the wall, a couple of sharp raps. Then she came out of the room so fast we could not help looking at one another—just an instant—though as soon as we had, I was sure we couldn't bear the look we exchanged, and she fled, I fled, but I remember the bruise under her right eye, about the size and color of a green olive. That was all I could remember at the time because I had to pee and because I ducked into the bathroom quickly to avoid the predictable appearance of the man who had hit her, in pursuit.

As I peed, I had the strangest feeling—that the woman with the olive bruise had known I was a boy under my falsies, gown, and wig . . . but the feeling soon passed, and when I returned to the bedroom, B. was tugging on the last arm of his creature suit, complete with green plastic scales, long razor claws, and large webbed feet. Seeing the huge, erect amphibian, gills poking out both sides of its head, its lipless, gaping mouth, I suddenly sensed that B.'s hairy arm protruding from the rubber suit seemed every bit as monstrous—or more—than the Swamp Thing itself . . . an odd juxtaposition. Then B.'s hollow voice came through the Gill Man's mouth. "Zip me up, for chrissake."

He raised and lowered his webbed feet and rotated awkwardly until I could get at the zipper. When he was zipped, I handed him his bag of genuine black swamp rot imported from New Orleans and some sphagnum moss he picked up at Dave's Bait shop outside of Fort Wayne, and we crept down the hall. I walked in front of the Creature, scouting, so no one would see us. Then we made our way around the perimeter of Tarnower's property to the finely cropped azaleas and hid behind them.

We watched and waited for Tarnower to give us the signal we'd agreed to beforehand. There was a faint odor of chlorine in the air, no one in the pool, the sound of the pool filter churning. Tarnower made a toast to Lily Fontaine, a local woman who had recently received an honorary doctorate for her career in charity fund raising, particularly for raising an enormous sum of money for the university in Fort Wayne. I took my position in the dark, near the spotlight, and the Creature continued to crouch behind the azaleas. When Tarnower finished his toast and various new accolades for Dr. Fontaine, hopes for his own daughter, well on her way since she'd now been presented to society and monied circles, and something about God, Rockefeller, Martin Luther, and Mad Anthony Wayne, he gave us our cue—

"And now a special performance," he said, "of a scene from a movie I'm sure you'll remember. . . ."

Tarnower doused the patio lights and B. reached a scaly hand out of the azaleas and put the spot on me. As usual there were a few "Ahs" for the banner, its dripping letters, then scattered and weak applause for me. I was picking azaleas (or pretending to, because the azaleas looked so fine I couldn't bear to actually pick them), then, suddenly the bushes shook and a deep primal growl came from them, ending in a kind of mournful howl. The Creature crashed through the bushes into the white conical domain of the spotlight, dripping with swamp rot and sphagnum moss hanging from its arms and shoulders. I tossed aside my imaginary bouquet of azaleas and, stunned by the Creature's gruesome appearance, I . . . well, here I should have screamed like my life depended on it, but even in weak light around the pool I saw from a corner of my eye the woman I'd passed in the hall on my way to pee—it happened so fast—she'd made-up the olive bruise, but the mascara had smudged, so that the whole area now resembled a ridiculous tear, like a clown might paint on her face. I stared at her. I saw her coming closer, at *me*, as if impelled by my presence, slowly, in a lethargic, frightening lumber, her arms slightly raised, like one of the Living Dead, like the Creature from the Black Lagoon himself! And this was not all that silenced me. Tarnower and his deb had come closer, too close, closer than ten feet, to *really* get their money's worth. He had his arm around her, protecting her, and her mouth was agape. I looked at Tarnower clutching his daughter, started to back away into the azaleas, then looked quickly back to the Creature, who stomped his foot in aggravation and growled again. Then, I believe out of a very different kind of terror, having nothing to do with not getting paid by B. or the frightful visage of the Creature, I glanced one last time at the woman with the botched tear on her face, put my willowy, white forearms alongside my head, stuck my elbows out, and SCREAMED. . . .

It was the best scream I'd ever made, so good I startled myself and felt for the first time in my career that my scream, long and shrill and rattling and pure, had been genuine, had scared *me*. Even the Creature looked a little shaken by it. He paused in his slow, relentless advance, clawed the air, then came on. As we'd practiced, I screamed again in shorter bursts, again . . . and again . . . then once more when the Creature took me by the throat and I tried with all the strength in my willowy arms to tear his death grip from my neck; then I fainted . . . and the Creature took me in his arms and carried me off, into the azaleas. . . .

We squatted in the bushes listening for Tarnower's guests to applaud, but they were silent, and we waited anxiously. . . .

"You either scared the living shit out of them," B. said through his creature head, "or you really fucked up."

Then there was a little scattered applause and B. went out to bow and I followed him to curtsy.

Later, getting our gear together, I asked B., "What do you mean I fucked up?"

"I mean, what are you doing looking at *them* like that?"

"It was a good scream—real."

"Yeah, sure it was. But *you're* not supposed to scare them, *I'm* supposed to scare them, I mean, the scene as a whole. . . . *I'm* the monster for chrissake, so look at me when you scream. *Me*! And you can't hesitate. It's all about the monster and the woman. It's kinda like Erica Jong says, it's the Zipless Fuck. That's what they're paying for, so you can't go looking at *them*!"

We were off until the next weekend when we had a job at the Snider High School Prom. B. had a soft spot for adolescents and horror, got very nostalgic at the prospect of doing a prom, kept talking about the golden age of the pubescent phantasmagoric: *I Was a Teenage Werewolf, I Was a Teenage Frankenstein, Teenage Monster, The Horror of Party Beach*, and whatnot.

B. sat on the workbench at his shop, dangling his stubby, hairy legs over the edge, working them back and forth. I listened as he reminisced, but all the while I kept thinking about my scream at Tarnower's the weekend before, the woman with the tear painted on her face—and my hesitation. Soon, the hesitation bothered me less than the scream itself. It wasn't the kind of scream I'd trained myself to make, full of fear and loathing, one that seemed to originate with something outside myself, the Creature. It was a scream that came from within, a hellish scream, the kind of scream that shocks the screamer, the way a baby screams until it's blue in the face, then pauses, first taken by the sound of its own scream, then frightened by it, and begins screaming all over again. . . .

We got to the high school about five, a couple hours before the prom, and found a boy's restroom because B. needed time to make himself into his Teenage Werewolf. He wanted to do something special, although he knew we'd only get about three-hundred bucks, half what Tarnower had paid us for *The Creature from the Black Lagoon*, a standard scene. B. wanted to do the Michael Landon werewolf, the scene in which the little horny, hypnotized, lupine hothead finds the girl wearing leotards working the balance beam in the gym—alone. I tried to explain to B. how difficult a scene with leotards would be—what was I supposed to do with my balls?

"Tuck 'em in," he smiled. "You know, stick 'em back between your legs."

I didn't know how to counter his proposal. The scene would be short enough, and I supposed they'd stay tucked in if I tiptoed on the balance beam with my legs together.

So we got ready. B. had the hardest time. He first applied a thin coat of brown greasepaint to his forehead and around his eyes. Then he sat in front of our portable vanity and tried to get all the tiny patches of horsehair to match his beard and stick to his face. We finally finished his wolf nose and fangs about seven-thirty, and he helped me attach the plastic flap of bloody skin to my neck—the one he'd tear open later.

We waited outside an inconspicuous set of double doors that led into the gymnasium. I heard the throbbing beat of the band and saw a strobe light flashing white, black, in the small panes of glass in the doors. I told B. I was going for a smoke since I knew it'd be at least fifteen minutes before our scene. I went out a door leading to a loading dock, lit my cigarette, took a couple drags, then heard a boy's voice below the dock:

"You know you want to."

And a girl's:

"How do you know?"

"I know."

"Leave me alone."

"You know you like it."

"I'll scream."

"No one will hear you."

I stepped on my cigarette and left the dock feeling terrible, cowardly. . . . Should I have stopped it? But how would *that* scene have gone? Were they lovers? Would they have both turned on me? As I walked back to the gymnasium, a girl ran past me in the hall. I saw her bare back cameoed in her sleeveless pink gown and a white ribbon trailing behind her in the air. Miss Tarnower, it seemed, having had her coming out only the week before, was now running from the loading dock. She glanced over her shoulder at me as she ran, making an awkward, frightened face—seeing me, it seemed, in my leotards, my embarrassing bulge showing through the spandex at my crotch. Then her date, a tall, handsome, dark-haired boy with what I considered an athletic square jaw, strode past me. He made long steps, pursuing Miss Tarnower, his pace somewhere between walking and running as though he wasn't sure he wanted me to know he followed her.

Back with B. I thought I had forgotten about Miss Tarnower and her pursuer, but when it was time to crown the Prom Queen, she was there on the platform, her blue eyes and fragile smile, her eyes lifted a little as her king, the mandibular athlete, lowered a glittering crown to her head that fit precisely over her blond bun, like a ring on a stub of finger. Suddenly the lights were killed, the band made a brassy flourish, and a spot shown on Miss Tarnower. She was radiant in the spot, her smile, the long delicate spears of light stabbing out from the cut glass in her crown into the gloaming of the gymnasium where all the dark shapes of young couples clung to one another in a kind of desperate yet detached astonishment of Miss Tarnower's beauty. . . . I was quite taken by her myself, then I saw the mandibular athlete, the King, what I took for his apparition in the shadows, just behind the Queen, smiling, his eyes lowered, his arms crossed over his chest.

Suddenly, the spot of light and the dazzling queen were gone. The prom-goers responded "Ahhh!" then giggled and rustled in the darkness. I heard the same voice I'd heard at the loading dock come over the PA system, "And now a little show, a slice of everyday life at Snider High." Then the spot went on me and the banner with runny lettering, I WAS A TEENAGE WEREWOLF. I tried to walk the balance beam, no small task. I focused my eyes on the beam and tiptoed gingerly along it, my balls inside my leotards hanging in back of me, and reminding myself . . . *not them, the Werewolf, no matter what, look at the Werewolf.* Another spot suddenly appeared, and the Teenage Werewolf sidled out the door and slowly toward me, stopping, dipping his head up and down, as dogs do, wearing red Keds with wolf hair poking out the torn toes and sides and eyelets. The Teenage Werewolf growled and howled and bared its fangs, salivating (for B. had arranged that, too). I bent forward at the waist (for my balls were coming out), slipped off the beam, and looked at the Werewolf, who suddenly went on all fours and began to lope in my direction, faster and faster. . . . Well, I could feel the usual scream coming from outside me, as it were, and readied myself to make it, but could not help noticing a door across the gymnasium where the Queen and King were now standing. I heard a sharp growl, glanced at the Werewolf, then back to the door, where the King was tugging at the Queen's arm, dragging her through the doorway; she had her crown in one hand and her heels to the linoleum, and she seemed to look at me as he lugged her through the doorframe—as if *I* could do something. . . . So I SHRIEKED at the highest octave I'd ever hit, pure and terrifying to me, even more so since the ceiling in the gymnasium gave it back with astonishing clarity and resonance. . . . Then the Teenage Werewolf tore my throat open and dragged me away from my balance beam, coughing and gasping, out the gym doors.

We stood outside the gymnasium and waited. The prom-goers were silent a long time, longer than Tarnower's dinner guests had been the week before. B. grew anxious.

"Well, this time you scared them shitless, kid. I mean you really scared them."

"Pretty good, huh?" I said timidly.

"Yeah, I guess, but Christ, they're just kids, kids in Fort Wayne. *Indiana*. Remember, it's supposed to be a *zipless* fuck!"

"What happened?" I asked him. "Did my balls slip out?"

"No, it's that scream of yours. I don't know what . . . and you gotta quit looking at them."

"I couldn't help it."

"Just look at me. I'm the monster, remember?"

I heard a smattering of applause through the double doors, then the gymnasium began to throb again with the vibrations of youth. No bow.

No curtsy. Later in the restroom, when we were packing our gear, B. seemed tired. He slowly unlaced his Keds, removed them from his wolf-hair feet, and set them aside. He seemed dejected, and I was puzzled how such a powerful and frightening scream could go so unappreciated.

My high school graduation was that week, so school was out for good. B. and I had a couple of days off, so I had no place to go, nothing to do. I wandered aimlessly around Fort Wayne. It was the lowest point of my career. I'd lost something, my touch, my voice—I didn't know what. The night before my wandering I had a nightmare that B. had come into my bedroom and used the "Italian Solution," as B. called it, to correct my problem, the way they made true falsettos in Italy. I remembered the nightmare vividly in the morning and tried to shake it off. As I lay in bed I looked at my undershorts and saw the reassuring lump there. Could *that* be my problem, I thought? No. I could still hit the high notes—too high. Was it some other change, a subtle shift in my body chemistry? What puzzled me most was that I had begun to make the most chilling screams I'd ever made, ones that I had a kind of faith in. I'd started to believe my part—and that, *that*, was possibly my undoing! I needed my old scream, one I could make at arm's length, direct at the monster himself, not the audience, a scream I didn't need to believe myself.

When I returned to B.'s shop on Coliseum Boulevard, he looked as though his last two days had been as bad as mine. His beard had grown over his entire face, high on his cheeks, and he looked a bit like his Teenage Werewolf without makeup. His bald spot looked pallid and white like the belly of a frog.

He was stirring blue and green greasepaint together in a tiny bowl, and I said, "Look, I'm sorry. Why don't you get someone else—maybe a woman."

He stopped mixing the greasepaint and looked at me. His eyes were shot through with tiny red veins and dark bags hung beneath them. "No," he said in a far-off voice. "Besides, I have a great idea. . . ."

B. explained that the Cinema Center people in Fort Wayne had their annual picnic that Saturday on the east bank of the Maumee River. They wanted something special, artful, so B. said we'd give them the '31 *Frankenstein*, the scene in which Frankenstein's monster, having murdered Fritz and Dr. Waldman, tramps through the countryside in a frenzied, confused state until he encounters a little girl by a lake who befriends him. The Monster sees the petals of a daisy floating on the water and, believing the little girl to be as beautiful, tosses her into the water, where she drowns.

"I'm not sure if the little girl screams in that scene," I said to B.

"I don't care if *she* does or not. *You're* going to scream. She screams, *then* she accidentally drowns, see? Like I told you—"

"I know. It's the payoff."

I wondered a moment if the Cinema Center folks in Fort Wayne, who B. called "those artsy-fartsies," would notice if we took liberties with the original scene, but B. said, "How long can you hold your breath?"

"I dunno . . . a couple minutes."

"Good," he said, "that'll do."

"You ought to get a little girl for this," I told him, thinking about how innocent, serene, and lovely Marilyn Harris looked in the original film.

"No. You'll do. Small bones. I'll be looking a long time for someone with lungs like yours—even a girl."

So we built the '31 Frankenstein to the specifications of Jack Pierce, the legendary makeup artist. I fitted B.'s head with a stiff rubber skull cap, one that looked like an overturned sauce pan. I puttied it to his head, pasted the hair on top, painted his face with blue-green greasepaint, applied plastic scars around the circumference of his head, and put two metal clamps through the rubber scars on each side of his forehead to hold them together. Then I made another long diagonal scar over his right eye, helped him into a five-pound steel spine, complete with a girdle and straps, and attached the big electrodes to each side of his neck. One leg at a time, he stepped into pants stiffened with steel struts sewn into the inseams, then his twenty-four pound asphalt walker's boots. I laced and tied the enormous boots, then slid a black, mildewy coat over his arms as he held them behind his back. I tugged the coat forward and buttoned it.

The last touches were a bit of putty around his fingers to fatten them, a bit of black shoe polish for his fingernails, and some black wax for his lips. I handed him two amber translucent contacts, alligator eyes, for him to pop in his eyes just before the scene. I left the Monster sitting on the workbench with his back to me, a silent, sorry looking hulk of metal, cloth, and greasepaint. *Befriend the Monster*, I rehearsed in my head, *then scream . . . befriend, scream, befriend, scream. . . .*

I slipped on my sundress printed with tiny roses, put a yellow ribbon in my wig, the one with limp, childlike blond hair, then put on a little makeup, no rouge or falsies for this scene, and a little lip gloss, dull and natural looking. I brushed my nicotine-stained teeth with a chemical whitener B.'d purchased, a concoction of peroxide and baking soda. I touched up my nose a little, stuffed daisies B.'d gotten at the FTD into the front pocket of my sundress, then got the Monster and guided him, each flat-footed step of the way, through the back door. I loaded him into the back of the van, got into the driver's seat, and headed for the Maumee River.

It was about mid-morning when I parked the van near a stand of willows by the Maumee. I opened the back of the van so the Monster could get some fresh air. I saw him sitting, his legs sticking straight out the back of the van like two stove pipes. *Remember*, I thought, *the Monster, look at the Monster. . . .*

I couldn't see his torso or face clearly, but I imagine he was grateful for the little bit of light and air I allowed him.

No one from the Cinema Center had arrived, though on a small knoll I saw the grills going in the pavilion. Smoke curled into the wooden vault above the grills and out the edges of the structure. The willows along the river cast deep green shadows over the water, which was smooth, ran out in an unbroken reflective sheet, and wound to the north behind a low hill dotted with houses.

I took the banner, reading '31 FRANKENSTEIN in B.'s characteristic drippy lettering, and tacked it to the trunks of two trees. Then I heard voices coming from the pavilion above. I ducked behind the van, then slid off into the willows. There, I saw two women in black, sleeveless dresses, staring out at the water, holding hands. They were lovely women with long, full black hair that ran to their waists. I remember how white and soft their exposed shoulders seemed, how tenderly each held the other's hand . . . *the Monster*, I remembered, *only the Monster* . . . .

I crept back around the rear of the van and helped the Monster out. I tugged at his stiff legs, and he helped me as much as he could by bending his knees and thrusting his arms back against the inside walls of the van. I helped prop him on the side of the van facing the water, away from sight.

When enough people had gathered in the pavilion, I turned to the Monster.

"Okay," I pointed at a spot about thirty feet in front of the van, "you go over there behind those willows. I'll take my spot under the banner in that little clearing by the river."

The Monster lumbered off, behind the willow branches. He put one leg in front of another, a sorry kind of goose step, his arms hanging at his sides. His head hung low. He seemed dejected as I watched him disappear behind the willows's umbrageous shapes.

When I saw that most of the people had gathered at the pavilion and were coming down the slope of the knoll, I sat under the banner between the two willows and arranged my sundress around me. I set my daisies nearby on the grass. It was calm, peaceful, the way summer mornings are, a calm I hadn't known in weeks, and I remembered the tender white hands of the women under the willow, then I lost my thoughts all together looking at the deep green reflections of trees on the water, then remembered, *no matter what, look* . . .

When the crowd gathered at the river, I continued looking at the water. I took a daisy and twirled it by the stem in my fingers. The director of the Cinema Center strolled briskly in front of the group and turned to address them.

"Now," he said, "B. Horror Enterprises presents a scene from the '31 *Frankenstein*—a scene you'll no doubt recognize. . . ."

The crowd was silent, then, unlike other crowds we'd played to, a general *hmmmm* rose from them, a kind of intellectual noise. Suddenly, the long tender osiers of the willows near me shuddered, and out came the Monster, his scars and blue-green paint so plain in the clear morning sunlight I almost gasped. He twisted violently at the waist around the five-pound metal spine. He flung his arms out and whirled them in the air like wild vanes of a windmill, ripping through the leaves of the willows and strewing bits of green all around. Then the Monster groaned, not a groan of menace or pure evil, but of confusion and desperation. I pinched the stem of the daisy in my hand.

The Monster spotted me and stomped the ground with his asphalt walker's boots, and I flinched thinking how good, how exquisite the performance was. . . . *No matter what, the Monster, this time only the Monster.* . . . Then the Monster's shadow came over me. His groaning dissipated into a gruff kind of curiosity. He knelt by me—and I looked at him. I looked into his alligator eyes, inhuman, yet filled with a cold sort of pain and frustration. I handed him my daisy. When the Monster took the flower in his enormous hand he grew silent, his expression perfectly serene; and I never once removed my gaze from his horrible features; then he reached for me, tenderly, gently . . . and, well, that was my cue to scream, but I couldn't. I was entirely taken with the sudden and extraordinary kindness of the Monster, his alligator eyes, what must have been his unfathomable pain, the perfect calm of the water. . . . I tried to scream. I opened my mouth but nothing came. The Monster whispered,

"Scream. . . ."

But no matter how I tried, I couldn't, and again through his black lips and from his alligator eyes set in his greasepaint and red plastic wounds, came the sound, "Scream. . . ."

But I still couldn't, so the Monster stood, and with a slight turn to the audience, grabbed me and growled, this time in anger, and put my head into the river, but I hadn't been prepared and water filled my mouth and nose and I recalled, *He isn't supposed to drown me on purpose*, I thought, *it's supposed to be an accident*; and when the Monster pulled me up, I coughed and reached up to secure a hairclip in my wig, and I heard him through the water draining out my ears again whisper, "Scream. . . ."

And he dunked me again in the river, pulled me up briefly, and then a third time dipped me in the Maumee, and when he brought me up I could barely breathe, my eyes bugged, I coughed, and my ears had filled completely with water. . . . Yet I could still hear a sound coming from somewhere. It seemed distant and unreal. The sound began at the topmost heart-rattling octave, the seed of a scream outside myself, a pure scream of desperation, of defiance—a woman in our audience was screaming loud and long, lonesomely, mournfully . . . but I never took my eyes off the Monster, even when his features were obscured by the Maumee as he held me underwater, even through the terrible division between air and water. . . .

B. fired me later, after we'd returned to the shop, put away our gear, and after he'd shed the Monster's coat and boots. He sat on his workbench near his spot-welding machine, his girdle and steel spine poking up. He rubbed his face with a towel and peeled off his plastic wounds.

"I gotta let you go, kid," he said, but he didn't say it angrily or with the least intimation of malice in his voice. And after that, he didn't say anything. I didn't say anything.

I helped him remove his steel spine and girdle. Then I left, thinking nothing would ever be quite the same between B. and me since my dunking in the Maumee. I left, closing the door on B. Horror Enterprises, left my high, frightening voice. I put my brilliant career behind me, my life ahead of me, a life in which I have rewritten the scene with the Monster, one I do my best to play over and over, though I'm never sure if I ever get it quite right. . . . In the scene I throw away B.'s creation and make a new monster, one from whom I never turn my gaze, one who hands me a flower, which I graciously accept. Then I give him a flower, lean in and kiss his great scar, kiss his black lips, put my arms as far around him as I can and hug him, hug his stiff, electrified, animated concoction of dead things. He feels big and sweet in my arms and strokes my hair with his blue, swollen fingers. Later, I undress him, remove every pretense, every dead and inhuman thing, every bolt, every strut, every electrode, every bit of plastic, his alligator eyes. . . . Then I turn my monster to the mirror and say, There, see yourself, you no longer need to be bewildered and afraid. . . . Is this not better? Better than what B. would have done with you? Is this not better than a woman's scream in a man no one will hear? Death by water?

MORTAL SINS

Jūratė, My Besmirched Bride,

If you can hear me from this far away, I'll try to explain. . . .

We are failed Catholics, if such a thing exists, if all hope for redemption and grace passed from our lives when we committed adultery while wedlocked to other persons now better unnamed.

Committed.

Do you remember how committed we were?

To adultery? So committed we committed the sin many times before we fell into the doubtful nuptial state we found ourselves in two years later, joined by the blessed, rock-solid hand of a Prudential insurance salesman from Akron who moonlighted as minister for the Unitarian church Mondays, Wednesday evenings, and weekends.

Remember how after the five-minute ceremony, we bought whole-life insurance, a piece of the Rock, and honeymooned at the Quaker Inn, a converted Mother Oats silo where, in a curio shop off the lobby, we stood for our wedding picture in the costumes of Bonnie and Clyde?

Romantic. Black and white and everything.

My Bespoken,

It didn't seem real. We were people of faith, real faith.

Oh, Holy Host, Body of Christ, American Dream, we swallowed you whole. Hocked ourselves to infinity. Got a place with space, maximum vertical space, tastefully defined by gypsum board and dark pressboard paneling, cathedral ceilings, inspiring and humbling at the same time, organic colors throughout, built-in home entertainment system with a front-loading twenty-four piece CD player for continuous music. Resonant, resplendent, organically-colored space and music, not too heavy, not too light, just right, siren of the Everlasting.

Remember?

I bought only the finest drapery for our little cathedral. I was a man of the cloth.

And such splendidly dressed space we'd never hoped to have with our mutual ex's.

At last!

We could believe all things moved toward one great goal: the divine manifestation of the paid mortgage.

We were pretty well off, right?

Broke every rule. Fucked ourselves religiously. By the Book. Divorced persons unnamed, which we always believed meant *de facto* excommunication from the Catholic Church.

We couldn't even say we were sorry.

Even if we meant it.

But Jūratė,

Remember our last ray of hope?

How our neighbor, Pascuzzi, dope-fiend and investment banker, proposed a solution? Offered to write a letter to the Pope in our behalf? Said he'd testify that the matters of our divorces had not been of our making (or making *it*, as it were), but had been the idea of our (betrayed) ex-mates all along. And how I told Pascuzzi, thanks for the offer, one mortal sin was enough, and I didn't wish him to blacken his pristine soul by having him bear false witness on behalf of ours.

Do you remember how it was?

Pascuzzi sat across from me at his breakfast table. He plucked errant hairs from his mustache. His eyes rolled up to gauge the height of his white, spackled cathedral ceiling.

"You sure, man?" he persisted. "I'm Italian. That should carry some weight with the Vatican."

"Yeah, but the Pope's Polish. Besides, I don't want to drag you into this."

"I don't mind," he said. He rolled a number, licked the paste along one edge of the paper, and smoothed the joint shut with his thumb and index finger. Then he ran his tongue lengthwise over it. "It's no trouble," he continued. "Really. I mean, I'd do the same for anyone whose souls were blighted for all time."

Stone Love,

Blighted for all time?

Pascuzzi lit the number and passed it to me. The smoke was yellow and sweet. A seed popped, and I suddenly felt relieved, certain I was doing the right thing by at least salvaging Pascuzzi's soul.

My Soul, My Everything,

When it comes to spiritual matters, I believe people should do everything to cut their losses.

Don't you agree?

So, I said, "It's okay, Pascuzzi. Really. We'll survive."

Besides, I reasoned, wouldn't His Holiness think it a bit suspect that Jūratė and I, joined in matrimonial bliss only five days after our divorces from our former spouses, were now asking to be reinstated in the Church at the same time and by the same benefactor? I expect no amount of pain in the eternal fires of Hell would have been worth the risk of such intellectual embarrassment. His Holiness may not think much of me in the long run—I mean so far as the Second Coming—but I'd be damned if I wanted Him to think I was an outright fool.

My Life,

Reason comes with passion. I believe that. No regrets.

Way I see it, reason doesn't pre-exist passion. You fuck, then say you're sorry; the other way around, nothing of any real consequence happens; nothing; besides, the Church buys this; coition, contrition; coition, contrition; in and out the confessional; in and out; a tedious cycle of grace and redemption.

But Jūratė,

You behaved as though passion came with reason.

Are you following me?

You had another plan, another ray of hope for our blackened spirits. This jag about Lithuania. You sat on the ottoman in our living room in your blue bicycle tights. You let your hair down, long, blond, straight, so it trailed along your back to the top of the ottoman. A pile of video tapes and CD's rose at your feet: a Fonda workout tape, some *Culture Club* stuff, my *Tears for Fears* collection.

"I'm taking all this over to GoodWill," you said.

"Not my *Tears for Fears*."

"Suit yourself."

"Those people at GoodWill won't want this stuff."

"Well, I don't either," you said. "I'm going to Lithuania to see the Gate of Dawn, *Aušros vartai*. I'm going to make a pilgrimage to Vilnius. I want to see the Pope when he comes. I want to find my ancestors, my great grandmother's house. I want to do it . . . do something."

So I responded, "You mean you're going to *Lithuania*?—as in Lithuania, eighty-five percent devout Catholic?—as in Lithuania, former Soviet Republic of—?—as in Lithuania, land of economic chaos and social unrest? A pilgrimage. The Real McCoy?"

And you said, "I've thought about it." You started to bite your fingernails, to lunch on your cuticles. I couldn't believe you'd go through with it. "I'll do good works there," you insisted, "make friends, try to get back into the Church. If God can forgive fifty years of official atheism, one little divorce should be easy."

"You'll have to become a saint or something," I said. "You gotta have at least four miracles, and I don't think the Vatican will count twenty pounds in two weeks on Deal-A-Meal as one. It's not like getting into the *Guinness Book of World Records*."

But you added: "I'll do it, you'll see."

So you stuffed the tapes and CD's into your father's old Navy duffle bag and handed me my *Tears for Fears* stuff.

I began to believe you were serious, couldn't let you go, didn't know why exactly, but also believed that a person, especially a person who carries an indelible black mark on her soul, should undertake new adventures with full knowledge of the consequences, so as not to blacken her soul further.

So, I asked you, "Do you know what you're doing?" I said, "I mean, let's examine your ancestry. Your mother's Welsh and Cuban; your father's second-generation Lithuanian-American, a devout Catholic by American standards, still eats fish on Fridays, a man who only last week found out that his sister was really his mother and his mother was really his grandmother because the person he thought was his sister was knocked-up out of wedlock.

"Big deal. It's not your fault. History is embarrassing. So what if your father's faith is shaken in God, Country, and Family, so he spends his nights at Jugs shooting pool and putting down beers. . . . And who cares if he found out his birth certificate was forged by his mother (really his grandmother), and his real birth certificate destroyed in a hospital fire in Pittsburgh in 1928?

"After all this, your father still wants to know the truth about his origins. But his grandmother, whom he thought was his mother, is no help because she's so senile she keeps calling 911, saying, 'There's a man in the house,' when it's really just him trying to talk to her to find out about his crazy roots."

"You're cruel," you said, and lugged your duffle bag onto one shoulder.

Cruel?

Me?

After all I just told you about your father and Fate and history and everything, I'm cruel?

I was desperate. I resorted to desperate measures. I hope you see that. I needed you to see how impossible redemption really was, so I kept talking. . . .

"The hell, you say," I said. "I care about you. I really do. I just don't want you to be let down. Don't you see how it is? Our eternal souls are damned because we committed adultery. Now, we could have continued to fuck all we wanted, having our steamy little affair, every now and then feeling the pangs of guilt, and confessing our sins and everything would have been fine. But we had to go and fall in love, right? So we divorced persons better unnamed and got married to put ourselves in the good graces of the State. But we no longer have the privilege of absolution. It's the old saw, Church versus State. It's the Thomas à Becket thing. Nothing to lose your head over. No reason to do anything drastic like flying off to Lithuania."

"Ha, ha," you groaned. "You might be wrong. I'll get back into the Church. It's changing, becoming more practical. And I want to see the Black Madonna and the Hill of Crosses at Šiauliai. I want to find my great grandmother's house."

"Aren't you confusing eternal salvation with who you are? Let's go to Puerta Vallarta. I hear the margaritas are better there. Aren't they getting a Disney World or something?"

But you and your duffle bag went through the front door, so I sat awhile on our bone-colored carpet with my neck cocked back. I looked a long while into the vaulted space above me, the flat blank color of bone.

Why hast Thou forsaken me? I thought. I'm not behind in my payments, am I?

Weeks passed. I became more desperate. What if you really went to Lithuania? People would say I couldn't keep a woman.

Jūratė Masonis,

You're the most pig-headed woman I have ever known. Kept your maiden name through two marriages, no big deal, a name which lost an 'i' when your great grandmother was processed at Ellis Island. Then you wanted to put the 'i' back, to make it "Mas*i*onis," legally speaking.

Remember how it was?

You were mowing our little condo-sized lawn, and I was walking beside you and shouted over the mechanical sputtering:

"All that PAPERWORK and legal MUMBO-JUMBO for an 'i'!"

"YES!" you shouted back, "and while I'm AT IT I'll try to get a volume DISCOUNT from the attorney on SEPARATION PAPERS!"

"The HELL!"

"Yeah, that's IT, the HELL!"

I went back to the chaise and watched you finish the lawn. Half, you did in vertical rows; then you switched and made concentric cuts; last, you changed to diagonal cuts. Back and forth. That's how it was. Back and forth. All ways, not one.

Cruel, Cruel Love,

It didn't seem real, how you cut the lawn so many ways and wanted a divorce all at the same time.

Sacred rituals?

And Lithuania.

I couldn't figure it. Maybe you regretted how your family lost so much land to the Soviets after the War. I thought you'd lost everything. I wanted to give you everything. . . . But I should have known better than to play you against your sister, the sort of rivalry that rivals the most profound and puzzling aspects of human nature.

"Hey," I spoke sweetly as you stood in the kitchen making a list of things to take to Lithuania—sweatpants, curling iron, vitamins, your Walkman. "I hear your sister's filed for divorce." I knew you hated Aldona, so I figured if I told you about Aldona's divorce, you might begin to feel contrary about getting your separation papers.

Go figure. I wanted you to stay with me.

So you asked: "Who told you that?"

"Aldona."

"Yeah? Where'd you see Aldona?"

"I was having a few beers with my friends at the IOOF Lodge, you know, Independent Order of Odd Fellows, and when I left I ran into her at the automatic bank teller. She looked like hell, wearing an Army surplus jacket, her hair all greasy and her eyes puffed—you know, how people look going through a divorce."

"What was she doing?"

"Looked like she was draining the account, kept sticking her card in the machine, punching $200, and stuffing the bills into her purse.

"So I asked her, 'What's up?' and Aldona said, 'I've filed for divorce. . . . I want to do something . . . anything besides what I'm doing, which is nothing, which is worse than anything. You know what I mean?'"

You know how she is, Jūratė.

So I watched for your reaction. You nodded yes. I went on.

"Aldona doesn't make any goddamned sense most of the time. She was talking to herself, not me. I think she's a bit unstable, her divorce and all. . . .

"Then I saw a twenty-dollar bill flutter down and land on the toe of Aldona's red pump, that's right, red pumps with an Army jacket, so I picked it up and told her that the twenty-dollar bill reminded me that I was hungry, so I asked her if she wanted to go over to the fish fry at the Catholic Charities at Saint Mary's. 'My treat,' I told her."

"I'll bet it was your treat," you said, and continued to fill your list of things to take to Lithuania: nail polish, Doctor Jane Reubens's *Herbal Medicine for the '90's*, assorted rosaries, blue, black, blood-red beads. . . .

Nothing worked. I planned to resort to most desperate measures.

I'd tell you I needed you. Wanted you. Could not live without you.

God help me, I'd say I loved you.

Sweetest,

Bear with me, okay?

The next day I found you sitting on the bed with dozens of pieces of amber strewn over the Pennsylvania Dutch quilt we'd gotten half-price at KMart.

"The hell," I said. "Where'd you get all this stuff?"

"I played the automatic teller," you replied, "to the tune of $800—then I went to the Penney's at the Mall."

"But—why?"

"Because my grandmother, Aurelija, told me a story about Lithuanian amber and me."

"Aurelija's bonkers. Amber and *you*? Give me a break. I'm leaving." I headed for the door, then stopped. "Go ahead, tell me the story.

I gotta hear this—it's amusing."

"Aurelija told me the story of Kastytis, a fisherman of the Baltic Sea."

"What kind of fish did he catch?"

"Does it matter?—fish," you said, "the kinds with gills and scales. . . . Anyway, one day while Kastytis was fishing in the Baltic he heard the voice of a mermaid named Jūratė. . . ."

"So you're the mermaid," I said. "How clever."

"Kastytis fell in love with Jūratė. But her father, Perkūnas, the Thunder God, was displeased because he and Jūratė were immortal and Kastytis merely mortal. So Perkūnas built a beautiful palace of amber beneath the sea, and filled it with all his servants and friends to persuade Jūratė to live with him. But Kastytis and Jūratė fell in love anyway—"

"Naturally," I said. I picked up a piece of amber and held it to the light coming through the double-paned bay window. A tiny fly was entombed in the amber, each delicate leg perfectly preserved. "I bet you paid extra for the bug," I said, set the amber on the bed, and turned to the door.

You said, "Do you want to hear this, or should I call a cab now?" I listened, but I couldn't look at you. "Well," you went on, "Kastytis took Jūratė to meet his mother, and when Perkūnas found out, he was so angry and heartbroken that he destroyed the palace of amber and with it Jūratė's immortality. . . . Jūratė's tears are the pieces of amber strewn along the beaches of the Baltic Sea."

I shouldn't have said it, but I did—I wasn't looking at you. I should have been looking at you when I said it.

"So, Jūratė," I said, "what are you going to do now—cry?"

And when I did look at you, you had been quietly crying all along. Queen of Amber,

Did you really believe Jūratė's story, or were your tears for me?

I waited until you went to Lithuania with your father and grandmother before I started tearing our belongings apart.

I wouldn't say I was shattered, just numb, unreal, that's all. One has to adjust to things. Deal with the pieces.

So before I started to take our belongings apart, I waited to get a letter from you. And when I did, a brochure was with your letter, printed in Lithuanian, the Hill of Crosses, KRYŽIŲ KALNAS, printed on the cover. It showed a mound of dirt with thousands of crosses of all sizes stuck everywhere at all angles, and smaller crosses and other religious symbols hung from the main crosses—pendants, rosaries, scapulars. You wrote that you made a large cross for your family, and smaller ones for yourself, your father, and grandmother and put them all on the hill—and you added that you had hung a cross for me, too.

If you can hear me from this far away,

Thanks. For nothing.

And you found the house your father's mother had been born in, but all that remained was a stone threshold and a weedy kitchen garden with stalks of dill sticking out and swaying in the breeze.

Jūratė,

How can you compare this mere threshold to the house we made together? Our little cathedral?

But you added that you could extend your visas because your father had found a job plumbing, and you'd found one teaching aerobics and cosmetology in Kaunas. You didn't know how long they'd let you stay, but you added that you'd been to see the Pope when he visited and spoke at the Cathedral in Vilnius. You said you wrote the Pope a letter in Polish with the help of your landlady, explaining everything, how you wanted to be reconciled with the Church, how you didn't know how to do it, and would he please explain to you how . . . and you handed the letter to a Lithuanian soldier and asked him to give it to the Pope.

Jūratė,

Passion without reason? Can it be true?

When I finished your letter, part of me knew that I'd have to separate our things, but another part of me knew once I'd done it the distance between us would suddenly become unfathomable, not like distance at all, but more like oblivion.

Can you describe the distance from one sort of oblivion to another?

Pascuzzi came over and helped me move all our stuff onto the front yard for a sale that weekend. I told him to put your stuff on the part of the lawn with the diagonal cuts, mine on the straight cuts, and yours on the concentric cuts.

Aldona showed, and I told her to take what she wanted. . . . I watched her, her surplus Army jacket, her brown hair bobbed, wander among your dresses, taking one up and holding it to her chest, then another, and another. . . .

Later, as the sun set, Pascuzzi sat on top of our dresser, his dark hairy legs and stubby feet working back and forth, swinging in the gloaming. He lit a number, then another, and strings of yellow smoke began to rise from the center of our belongings and float above us in a stale plume against an invisible ceiling.

My Bride Besmirched,

If you can hear me from this far away, bear with me—I'll try to explain. . . .

After a little while, I wondered why you hadn't mentioned finding the Black Madonna in Vilnius in your letter, and here it got darker and darker until I could barely make out the forms of Aldona moving among your things or the smoke rising from Pascuzzi's joint from the middle of our belongings scattered about the lawn, and after a time I could only see the tiny red ashen end of something glowing in the dark, until in the blackness I could no longer imagine that any of this, the pieces of our second go at redemption, pieces of our little cathedral, had ever really existed, had come from any place at all, and I believed none of it existed, you never existed, as I believed nothing before in my life, and I had faith in this, a faith I hope you'll never know, a faith in feeling nothing at all, because reason needs passion, and the mortal souls of the damned have no tears. . . .

Dark Lady of My Dreams,

Remember the way we were in our hours of need?

Later, Pascuzzi called over to me as I was sorting through the CD's. "You want me to write that letter to the Pope?—the one about you and Jūratė?"

"No, Pascuzzi," I said, "what you going to do?—write one for me?—then Aldona?—those others who shall remain nameless?—and after that?—imagine all the letters you could write."

I heard Pascuzzi whisper, "The hell, you say."

"Yeah," I said. "The hell."

Day Cook

First customers leave little mounds of paper cups and steel platters piled with fatty strips of unregarded steak and bone. It's too early to watch the clock, so I go into the dining room, straighten a few benches, and bus tables. I have a smoke by the coffee warmer. I resist looking at the clock a long time, then glance at it. Eleven-twenty. Time. Not much else matters.

I think of Kostos, a wiry, thick-lipped guy I used to know. After I got off my shift, he'd come into the Rawhide Steak House and we'd walk back to my new apartment, past our old elementary school playground. Kostos said the only thing wrong with the world was that it cost too much to extract salt from sea water. He built his seaside electrolysis plant word by word as he pushed me in circles on a green, wood-slated merry-go-round. The muscles in his freckled face palpitated, his arms stiffened against the boards. He raced alongside the spinning contraption, then slipped away. He stood with his hands on his hips, smiled with satisfaction as I whirled by his image, frame-in, frame-out, fractions of trees, bushes and power poles, the auburn brick in the schoolhouse elongating in perfect streaks around me, then shortening as I slowed.

Then Kostos jumped onto the merry-go-round; he sat by me saying something about all that fresh water growing crops and feeding people. And beginning the next syllable, he said he had some saltpeter, sulfur, and charcoal. *Could we make a bomb? Could we explode it across the railroad tracks behind my apartment complex?* I never thought much about sea and salt and world hunger, but we both understood bombs—and how I lived better than most guys, me having a full-time job. Kostos said I live beyond my means, easy for him to say because he was stuck with a crummy paper route, and another year at Valley Forge High. But I got out of Valley Forge, got my own place.

Nat Tabb, Franchise Manager of this Rawhide, stands in the doorjamb of his office; he's an ex-San Bernardino cop, still has that kill-me-if-you-can swagger, an enormous handgun he keeps on top of the safe in a Muriel cigar box; sometimes when he figures I'm not moving the line fast enough he pokes the gun's barrel out the door of the office, just a couple inches, that huge front sight poking up like a black sail; but now I see smoke running in white strings out the office door; he's having a smoke, too, giving me his heartless grin, the one he beams when he knows I know the place is empty, when he knows I know I'm not earning my keep. But this is Days, slow, so we both expect it.

If you come to Rawhide, you can get a ribeye, fries, and salad with your choice of dressing—all for a lousy $4.19. Cream pies and coffee are extra. Most people say, *How can you sell it so cheap?* I tell them it's a mystery of free enterprise, one of those secrets you get to know if you're Day Cook.

"Want an application?" I ask them.

They laugh and waggle their heads *no*; I suppose they're happy to know they may have gotten a good deal. Maybe they have. Most of the gristle in these ribeyes is pretty delicate, and a little gristle they'll put up with, along with brown fringes on the salad, *but let their meat be bloody*, and the devil in them gets out and dances on hot fires.

"Kill it!" some of them screech.

"I can't eat this dog meat!" others lament.

One regular customer wears black horn-rimmed glasses and stands at the order station, holding his plate out at me with his half-gnawed steak on it. He lays his head on his shoulder in acute disappointment and says,

"Well . . ." just like Jack Benny.

I know it's a lot to put up with, but it beats being out in the world. I used to have to be out in the world. When I was Dish Boy, Tabb made me go outside—to pick up the parking lot.

"Isn't it heavy?" I asked him.

"Wise ass," he snarled. "Pick up the cigarette butts and paper cups and styrofoam and shit like that," he said, "outside—all of it—every day."

Picking up customers' shit in the parking lot, that's how I came to know all about the world and about doubt—I wonder if just once I could convince a customer who orders everything burned that there's a kind of awful beauty in a medium rare, something glorious about blood running freely. . . .

But I'm no artist. I cook them how they want them. And I'm glad to do it, to be here on Days, though the Old Man says Days at the Rawhide aren't real life. The Old Man says someday, if I'm not careful, I'll find out what real life is. Such nonsense. The Old Man has worked Nights half his life and Graveyards the rest, so he thinks he's some kind of expert on suffering. He says I should go back to school. College. For what? To learn *nights*? I have Days now and I'm keeping them. That's a sure thing.

And I'll probably never give Days up. Look at Kostos, what he risked. . . . He used to listen to his parents. He got good grades. He worked early mornings on his dumb paper route to save for college. One morning he didn't come home. Then he didn't come to school. His mom even called me at the Rawhide. After my shift, some kids found him behind my apartment the other side of the railroad tracks, hanged by his neck with a plastic jump rope tied to sapling bent over like a parabola. A stupid parabola. They don't teach that kind of geometry at Valley Forge.

People started saying things about Kostos, how he didn't mean to do it to himself, how he was jacking off and choking himself at the same time, trying to create a kind of euphoria, and lost track of time. Others say it might have been murder. Detectives wanted to talk to me.

I met them at the Principal's Office at Valley Forge. First, the detective with yellow paisleys on his necktie whispered something to the one with tiny, jumping dolphins on his necktie; then the one with dolphins nodded at me.

"He's the Best Friend," he said.

The detectives had a small, shiny black recorder going on the desk. We talked awhile, real friendly, almost like Kostos hadn't done anything to himself, like everything was perfectly normal, and when I couldn't stand it anymore, I asked the detectives, "Well, do you guys think he was jacking off, or not?"

They laughed.

How could they laugh about something like that?—I mean, I can see laughing about jacking off, and maybe laughing about death, each separately. But together? Isn't that something all together different?

Days aren't real life? Bullshit. Real life isn't real life.

Ask Kostos.

I drop my burning butt on the floor and flatten it with the toe of my boot. I twist the butt into grout between floor tiles for Tabb's benefit, and I see him start for me, scowling, so I kneel, scoop the butt in my hand, and carry it in back, thinking it may be the best laugh I'll have all day, how time moves so slow on Days, how it moved a little too fast for Kostos.

Tabb joins me at the broiler. He runs at the mouth about me as if I were something special, but I'm thinking the reason is that I'm eighteen and available to work days. Most kids aren't.

"It's hard to get legal help these days," he says.

"Remember that," I say, "next time you're giving raises."

Since I left Valley Forge, all the high-schoolers who work here think I'm some idol of adulthood. There's the Bus Girl who's barely two weeks from graduation. She says she wants to work Days, and I keep wanting her to want to work Days with me, full-time. But after leaving Valley Forge, most like her, the good ones, go off—somewhere. Some to colleges. But they can't all go to college. Can they?

Who knows where they disappear? Nunneries—some such places.

The telephone rings and Tabb goes to the far end of the line and gets it. Then he stands at the register with the receiver tucked under his chin. He hangs up and he's banging register keys, totaling the first hour's receipts. Typical first hour. A bad one. I could do the receipts in my head, but Rawhide Corporate Headquarters in Dayton wants Tabb to call in hourly readings, so he does them on the register just the same.

A customer comes into the chute. He looks like he's had his nose broken a couple times, and he wears a gold choker that snakes through thick hair poking out the deep vee in his pink silk shirt. Sometimes, I'm amazed how long people like this guy study our platter menu. There are four lunches—ONE through FOUR—and TWO is the ribeye special. Simple math. Come on, I'm thinking, get your ass up here and order. I need another smoke.

The man walks up the chute and orders a T-Bone—a ONE—and an orange drink. I tell him it isn't the Special, I'll have to cook it from scratch; he says it's okay, he has plenty of money and plenty of time.

The man sits in the dining room and sips on his orange drink. Tabb walks to the broiler, slips his hands in his front pockets, studies the grill, and says, "How'd that guy order his steak?"

"Well done."

"Good," he says, "put it on a low heat grate."

Soon, two men in tacky plaid suits (one, blue-green; the other, brown-orange) come in the front door. They walk up to my customer, who's still sipping his orange drink; each takes one of his arms; the two men yank him to his feet and muscle him out the front door.

Tabb comes back to the broiler, slips the customer's steak onto a platter, sets himself up with a knife, fork and A1 Sauce, and heads for his office to eat it. He glances sideways at me, just as he passes the cash register.

"Cops," he chuckles and ducks through the door with the T-Bone.

Later, Tabb tells me the man's been in before, night shift, just at closing. He says the *Son of a Bitch* robbed the store, locked the whole night crew in the bull pen, then fried himself a T-Bone, ate it in the dining room, and left with the night's receipts.

"The nerve," Tabb huffs. "He robs me, then in a couple weeks he comes right back in, big as you please, and wants himself a nice lunch." Then he gives me that grin. "Too bad I wasn't around when he robbed us. I'd have offered him one of them Muriel cigars, know what I mean?"

We're filling up pretty good with the lunch bunch. The chute's jammed and Tabb's running the salad station. He plucks the lettuce and purple cabbage leaves around in the wooden bowls, arranging them in balanced portions of color.

He grins at each customer.

Behind me, I hear fragments of speech, *French*, and *TWO*, and *FOUR with fries*, then, *Mister Tabb, you make them pies yourself?*

"Sure do," Tabb lies to them.

I'm laying more meat than I need on the grill. I know the mix. TWOs and FOURs. Fries and bakers. Orange drink. French. Italian. Thousand Island.

"How would you like your steak done?" I hear Tabb say.

"Well," a man replies. "Well, well, well! No pink. Not one micromolecule of blood. White. Dry inside. Well done!"

Tabb shouts back to me, "Burn it!"

A familiar haze begins to gather over the grill, rising and racing out the overhead power vents.

Days are easy, I'm thinking. I've got them down to an art. Well, if not an art, maybe something like it? I mean, I don't have to think about Days anymore. Like Days are pure feeling. But are they? I mean, I'm cooking and I'm not thinking about anything, just the mix, the time, busy time, the lunch rush, pure feeling, just like the *Rawhide Day Cook Manual* says: *Never cut a steak to check its doneness. Never let it bleed. Instead, check its doneness by how it feels, by the touch of the meat with your tongs, the time it lays on the hot grates, its texture to the eye.*

And then there's the unwritten motto of the Day Cook:

IN RAWHIDE WE TRUST.

It all comes with experience. After a time, I don't have to ask how they come together—time, touch, and texture—it's all somewhere hidden from me, all in the busy time, feeling without thought, Day Cooking. But it's so hard to have faith in time, touch, and texture, like they'll all come together on their own, like it's really possible to *know* the moment they come together, moment everything's done to perfection. Then I wonder a little about the Bus Girl who wants to switch over to Days. I wonder if she's cherry. Then I think, Who cares? Nothing's cherry anymore. I wonder if Kostos ever had a girl before he strangled himself jacking off and forgot about time, that plastic rope around his neck.

Tabb comes back to cook and I take the salad station awhile, and I remember the time I was tossing a man's salad; I covered it with French and blue cheese together, handed the bowl to him, and when I looked up he had *disappeared*. I went to the other side of the line, and the man was lying on the floor near where I'd been tossing his salad. He was dying of a heart attack. He had salad all over his face, which was blue under the red French, blue cheese, purple cabbage, green iceberg lettuce; his lips were white, and all I could think was that these couldn't be the colors of death; they were absurd, like color TV before they perfected it.

Later, Tabb and I could hear the ambulance howling outside, taking the dead man away. Tabb came up to me. He grinned ear to ear, saying, "How am I supposed to survive if you keep killing my customers during Lunch Rush? If you wanna kill someone, kill them in Dead Time."

Since Kostos choked himself to death, the heart attack was the first calamity I had on Days, and it should have shaken me, but now I think if the guy fell over and kicked-off on my lunch line, I'd be happy to carry him to the curb to keep my line moving, to keep the "level of service up," as Tabb calls it.

Time, touch, and texture. Not much else matters.

Tabb and I kill the line and since I'm in Dead Time now, I have another smoke. My smoke is good and customers begin to leave, the parking lot begins to empty, customers' cars flash by the checkered curtained windows in the dining room. I hear the metered squeak of the front door as they exercise it open and closed.

I run water from the fountain cooler over my cigarette, then my face. I walk over and pitch the butt in the *THANK YOU* pail by the front door. I go back to the broiler and begin to wipe down the stainless steel with some stuff call Blue Satin.

When I stash the Blue Satin, my first customer in Dead Time comes in. It's Mr. Hope again. I ask him what he wants, and he drops to his knees, holding his fingers out in front of himself, like he's pinching something, and whistles at his imaginary dog. "Here, boy! Here, good doggie! Here, boy!"

Tabb comes out of his office, folds his arms over his chest, and leans against the coffee station. He watches Mr. Hope, who's still on his knees, and who thinks he's Bob Hope's brother. I must admit he looks a lot like Bob Hope, and this *is* Cleveland, where Hope was born. Or was it London? Still, seeing the man on his knees, whistling at an invisible dog, I get used to calling this loony bird *No Hope— No'pe.*

"Get him out of here," I say to Tabb.

"Nope," he says. "His money's green."

Tabb whistles a line from "El Paso" and walks into his office.

Two more regulars appear in the chute. The first guy owns the Sun filling station across the street. His brother is in jail for breaking and entering. He's having a FOUR—chopped beef—with mushroom sauce.

The guy behind him drives a Wonderbread truck and I always marvel at how neatly he dresses for having such a dumb job. He wears a smartly pressed white shirt, and a tie with an Olympics tie clasp poking through the split lapels of his Wonderbread work blues. He wants a TWO and he's in a hurry.

I'm watching the clock over Tabb's office. I hear the night crew kids in back, laughing and shoving each other around, tying their aprons, cutting spuds, getting ready. Dead Time's almost over. I *must* be the lucky one. I got out of Valley Forge.

Then a woman steps into the chute behind the Wonderbread man. She wears a black pillbox hat with a short gray veil that cuts her face in half, like a fog bank. She gives me the creeps, but I don't know just why. I've never seen her in here before.

She orders a TWO, studying my face as she speaks, then she breaks down, sobbing behind the veil. Her dinner tray hits the floor with a slap; I drop a nice-looking ribeye on the floor at my feet.

It's Kostos's mom. I barely recognized her.

Tabb comes out of his office and smiles painfully at the other customers. He walks to Kostos's mom, helps her stand on her own, then leads her out the front door. Then he walks behind the line to the broiler. I brace for one of his wisecracks. But luckily he's not smiling; he's looking at the floor, at the raw red ribeye, and he falls to his knees, taking the meat in his hands and, almost lovingly, carries it in back, into the kitchen.

Sometimes Tabb can be damn touching, like maybe there is something behind every heartless smile he ever gave me in Dead Time. But now he comes back, smiling his wicked smile.

"Don't worry about that ribeye," he says in a low voice.

He says he'll brush the meat off, use it on night shift, it'll be good as new, and, *by the way, could I provide janitorial services every day?* He wants me to think about it, then says he's raising the price of TWOs next week to $4.29, and maybe I'll see a little more in my paycheck. I ought to tell Tabb it's never enough. But I know it's always a sure thing. I'll take what I can get. The rest's a mystery. So I'm not asking any questions—

Time, touch, and texture.

Never cut anything.

Never see if it bleeds.

WHO MADE YOU

Trudy is sitting like an Indian, powwowing with her Greenpeace papers. She wears green Bermuda shorts, white tube socks pulled up to her kneecaps, one of my T-shirts, and no bra, which has never been an event around our house since her breasts are pleasing, but not overly ample. . . . Sometimes I wonder if she sees them that way too. Her skin is pasted to the cotton shirt with sweat. Trudy rocks forward and back; she pulls one paper from a pile, then lays it on another. Other papers are strewn about the living room carpet. It's like a crazy kind of solitaire. This is something she takes very seriously: the bigger the mess, the more serious the environmental matter. It's her *outside* interest. So I don't mind her spreading out in the living room. She seems really hot, like me, but she looks strangely comfortable with her papers all around her.

I bring my toast and coffee into the living room and I sit on the couch, directly over Trudy's shoulder. It's hot this summer. I mean *hot*. It's a heat that comes from wherever the ultimate furnace dispatches heat. It's beginning-and-end-of-time hot. It's *romantically* hot, I tell Trudy; but she doesn't believe me. I can tell by the way she keeps her back to me, square, below and slightly in front of my knees. If I move, she moves. I'm not sure she wants me to see what she's reading.

There are flies in the house. Fat ones. The ones that seem aerodynamically unstable, or impossible, like owls or moths or DC-10's.

One fly makes an unsteady approach to the title page of Trudy's report on "Biological Degradation of Organic Compounds." She brushes the fly away and huffs.

I suppose Trudy's *inside* interest is cosmetics; she sells them at the May Company. That's her job. I've been out of work. It's been so long I don't care. It's kind of incredible, but Trudy and I are getting by. When you work for someone, they want you to believe you could never make it without them. The fact is you can, for awhile.

I tell Trudy I'm trying to get rid of our refrigerator. But it doesn't have anything to do with the heat, not really. It hums and clicks loudly all the time. I notice it mostly at night when I'm trying to sleep. If I don't sell it, I'm going to junk it; but we could use the money; so I'm trying to sell it first. I mean I'm not trying to screw anyone by selling it. It works okay. But it's old: it's probably near the end of its useful life. I just don't want it to conk out before I sell it; all the meat will thaw, then rot, then smell, and I'll have to get rid of *it* too.

I tell Trudy last week I ran a free ad in the *Enterprise* about the refrigerator. The ad reads like this:

> *Refrigerator, frost-free, 15 cubic feet, Admiral; dual refrigerator/freezer temp controls, meat keeper, crisper, $125. 738-7403.*

I'm not sure she hears any of this, but I tell her the Admiral didn't sell last week. I got a couple of calls, one from a lady who wanted a refrigerator, but she wanted it to be colored harvest gold. The other call was from a man who needed one for his father, who was very old and very sick—the man couldn't come to pick it up, and he said he could only give me $75 for it.

This week, I tell Trudy, I ran across a nifty item in the *Enterprise*, quite by coincidence: the item is about refrigerators. I found it in a column called "Mr. Fix," by a man named Dan Fixx:

> *There are some very important do's and don'ts when it*

*comes to transporting your refrigerator. If your unit does
not have casters, I recommend tilting the unit up and insert-
ing pieces of carpet scrap on the sides, under the front and
back of the unit. Please remember if you are discarding a
refrigerator unit, you must remove the doors to prevent a child from
crawling in and locking himself in the refrigerator. This type
of tragedy happens more often than you realize.*

I'm thinking I wouldn't want a tragedy to happen. I figure I'm
going to need a reminder. I cut out "Mr. Fix" from the *Enterprise* and
fasten it to the outside of the freezer door with a magnet. Then I go
back and sit on the couch to watch Trudy.

"I'm going to Columbus for a Greenpeace rally," Trudy says, and
she walks off into the kitchen. She calls from there, out of sight.
"Norma's picking me up."

I call back to her: "Don't you think these are things you should
know? I mean, that one about removing the refrigerator door is pretty
good, huh?"

"Jesus," she says. I hear her running water into a glass. I get up and
look into the kitchen. She tips her head back, breathes, and downs the
water.

"Some day I might not be around, and you'll need to remember
this stuff I read to you."

Trudy puts her hands on her hips. She smiles. "I *know* things," she
says.

I know what those things are Trudy knows. I know we're about to
play her favorite game, a distorted version of a televised game show:
Jeopardy Catechism. "Go ahead, ask me: *Who made me?*" she per-
sists. "I'll show you how much I know."

"Okay Trudy. . . . Who made you?"

"God made me. . . . Go on, now ask me another one, ask me *Who
is God?*"

"Then, Who is God?"

"God is the maker of Heaven and Earth."

We both laugh—and once again Trudy swears to me the queries and responses are almost exactly as the nuns prescribed them when she was a little girl. She tells me how the kids at Saint Margaret's were quizzed daily, just like that. . . . I guess it's the sense of real history, so close and personal, that makes it so funny.

Trudy changes into her jeans and a tropical top, a blue-green shortsleeve with flamingos all over it. Norma's car pulls in the drive and I hear the horn toot once, then a couple more times in succession, staccato. I kiss Trudy at the front door. She slings on her backpack, which is gorged with the papers that had been strewn in the living room.

"*No* watering the lawn, okay?"

"All right," I say, "but only if you answer me this . . ."

Trudy is smiling again; she waves at Norma's car and turns back to me. I am glad to see her smile. She rarely smiles on the verge of a Greenpeace rally.

"What is it?" she asks.

"Who are the *Devils*?"

"A devil," she says obediently, "is a bad angel. The bad angels would not obey God, so they were not allowed to be in Heaven."

"Get outta here," I say, and I push her through the door.

The town is heating up fast. I go out the back door of the house and walk to the garage. It's only about 10 a.m. and the air is steamy, suffocating. I'm conscious of my own sweat. My garbage smells. So do my neighbors'. It's hard to tell whose garbage is whose, or whose is smelling worse—or smelling more distinctively—since the summer has been such a hot one. The whole neighborhood reeks with garbage, just the way garbage smells as a whole, I guess.

I go to the side of my garage and look at my garden. It's July and nothing's up. The clay is desiccated, fissured; my garden looks like a lunar landscape.

Frosty, the neighbor who lives behind me, comes out of his back door; he walks to his small garden in the back corner of his lot. He bends regretfully at the waist, inches his bifocals up the bridge of his nose with his forefinger, and inspects several rows of limp green onions. I have seen Frosty many times this way; even on dog days like this, he wears a crisp, starched white shirt and a blue tie with a tight, tiny knot at the top, along with button-sized, onyx cuff links; he's kicking at the dust in his garden with his brown wing tips.

Frosty's retired from the Air Force. He's married to a woman named Violet. She wears full-length navy blue polyester dresses, and heavy brooches on them that hang cockeyed from her flat chest, and tug the material into permanent little peaks where the pins go through. Frosty comes over to me. He stands in my driveway and takes out a handkerchief. He pats his forehead and neck with it.

"Does your garbage smell as bad as mine?" he asks me.

This is Frosty's way of getting me to admit what I already know. I know this because I know Frosty pretty well, so I don't mind. My garbage smells as bad as the next guy's. True, sadly true. But I don't mind his asking. I like Frosty, the way he asks his questions, the sense of leveling about them. He always includes himself in any derision, or any hint of something rotten, like some of the things he has asked over the years: "Your feet hurt as bad as mine?" or "Your onions as sick as mine?"

So I say, "Probably worse."

"Say, where's the missus?"

"At a Greenpeace rally."

"She's pretty serious about that stuff, isn't she?"

Frosty smiles as he asks his question, so I am forgiven ahead of time for not responding. He goes back to his garden. He kicks at the dust between his onions.

I go back inside the house. Frosty stays with his onions. I clean out the refrigerator in case someone wants to come over right away to see it. I throw out some old stuff: limp celery, oranges growing penicillin on them, bottles with tacky bottoms. I microwave a burrito. I watch Frosty circle his garden. I imagine a slow, grinding dirge playing, a solitary mourner. Suddenly, Frosty snags a weed, hauls it up and flings it into my yard. Then he looks around to see if anyone is watching, then walks into his garage. Violet comes out and stands on her back porch. She's watching the neighborhood, like a woman standing guard. A black, spiny, 1920's brooch hangs in the middle of her chest; it seems close to tipping her over the porch railing. Frosty comes back with a mayonnaise jar filled with water. He tips the jar twelve times over his onions. There are twelve dark spots in the lunar landscape. I watch them fade, evaporate.

Trudy comes in the front door. She walks into the living room. I hear the couch sag. I go to see her; she gets up and swaps her backpack for a leather briefcase, pours the papers out of it onto the floor, and wades into them.

"I have to go over to the K of C now—I'm late."

Trudy means she has a *N I M B Y* meeting—the club for people who don't want hazardous waste dumps anywhere: *Not In My Back Yard. NIMBY*. Pretty nifty, I think sometimes. I like acronyms; sometimes they tell us things about the cause they represent. There is no such word as *nimby*, but it has a great sound. Jack be nimby. Jack be quick.

"You have a meeting?"

I don't know why I ask her this. I already know. I guess sometimes it's just good to check. For example, what if Trudy responded:

"No, it's not a meeting—actually, these piles of paper are the various motions I'm filing for divorce."

Naw, I think. That's pretty crazy. But I guess it's good to check every now and then.

So, in fact, she responds to my inquiry:

"So?" she says.

"So," I say, "have fun."

I open a copy of the *Enterprise*. A joy. It's really a great newspaper. You can advertise anything free for 20 words or less. Last summer I sold some firewood and a coffee table in the *Enterprise*. This summer the firewood I have left probably won't sell. It's too hot. We've had three months of drought here. Everybody's going nuts, so the radio and TV say, but you don't see people out going nuts, you only hear about things being crazy, or read about them. But not in the *Enterprise*. It's not that kind of newspaper, not given to exaggeration or speculation. Just practical things. Practicalities.

Anyway, these articles in the *Enterprise* are pretty good stuff for improving the general human condition. The only problem with the *Enterprise* is you have to wash the ink off your hands when you're through with it or you'll sneeze.

"You got a minute?" I ask Trudy. "Okay if I read to you?"

"Okay," she says, pulling a staple from a blue-jacketed groundwater quality report.

"Okay . . . you ready?"

"Okay, let's have it."

"Then here's the first one: *The Ice Cube Trick.*"

> *Ever want just one cup of fresh coffee, but don't want to brew a full pot? We use "coffee cubes." Simply brew a pot of coffee and pour it into one or two ice cube trays. Carefully place the trays into the freezer. Then, when you are ready for a cup of coffee, put a few cubes in a cup and heat it in the microwave. Stir occasionally. In about two minutes you'll have a cup of hot coffee and it still tastes fresh!*
> *—Jean C, New York, New York.*

Trudy stands and walks around her piles of paper; she bends at the waist and inspects them.

"Well—what do you think?" I ask her.

"*The Ice Cube Trick* sounds like a waste of energy," Trudy says, then she adds, "—remember to take that stuff in the garage to the recycling station in Spenserville today."

"Okay . . . hey Trudy."

"Huh?"

"Who are the Saints?"

Trudy takes her brown ropy hair in both hands, pulls it back and ties it in a pony.

"The Saints," she mumbles, "that's a good one. . . . Oh, yeah . . . the Saints are people who have suffered for being good—so God makes a special place in Heaven for them."

I'm playing with her breasts now.

I say: "I know that *Saints* one always turns you on, Trudy."

"No," she laughs.

"Come on."

"No. I gotta go. Don't forget that stuff in the garage."

I go in the side door of the garage where I keep the empty paint and paint thinner cans, pesticide bottles, and used motor oil in plastic jugs. I put these odds and ends in a box, carry them to the car, and put them in the trunk. I push up the garage door and wait awhile, considering my chore: my trip to the recycling plant.

I get in the car, start it, back down the drive onto the street, make a right, then another right onto the county road: COUNTY ROAD 501.

The air is dead and the sky shocked deep blue from horizon to horizon. I don't see a cloud in sight.

After awhile I drive past *Auglaize Acres*, a rest home. East of the rest home, on the right side of the road, the huge, white, humped back of the county dump rises above a thin stand of poplars. Zillions of white birds carpet the slopes of the garbage dump: some fly up—leaping like winged-and-feathered frogs—and relight on the trash, so the white carpet is in continuous motion, an undulation, like spasms under one's skin, a boiling white down, a rancid molting.

I pass an abandoned farm house, then a field of cut winter wheat and two stands of field corn, which by now should be tasseled: but this corn is pea-green; its blades are thin and witchy—it looks like acres of yucca plant, not corn.

I pull off County Road 501 and take the State Route into Spenserville. I turn into the graveled lot at the Recycle Station. Dust boils up behind the car, then the dust cloud doubles back, engulfing my car. I hold my breath. I wait for the cloud to pass; I watch it move off behind me, to the State Route where it hangs over the road. Then the haze, shaped like a big-fisted hand, crosses the pavement and disperses into a bunch of trees. I get out of the car, open the trunk, and carry my stuff to the recycle station office.

A man comes out of the office before I make it to the door. When he opens the door, hundreds of flies take off, circle and reland on the door as it shuts. I've never seen so many flies. He's a new man at the station; he's thin, wears heavy faded jeans—not prewashed, faded truly from use—and a T-shirt with the caricature of a white-faced pit bull dog on it. His boots are daggered, the toes of the boots sharp to the point of being dangerous, potentially painful, even to look at. The new man has long teeth, a full head of hair, and he's smiling; yet as I walk closer to him I realize that he is not *truly* smiling: his mouth is configured like a smile, but it does not convey the emotion that corresponds to a face that is *smiling*. Rather, his lips are drawn back over his teeth, and the bridge of skin between his nose and upper lip is curled; he's breathing with that twisted expression, breathing through his long teeth.

"How's business?" I say.

"I wouldn't know," the man says. "I'm new. I'm on contract here. . . . They just went to all-contract people last week—you got something for us or not?"

I raise the flaps up on the cardboard box I'm holding. I point to the cartons of used motor oil, then the empty paint and thinner cans.

"That's all?" he says with disgust. Then the man who breathes through his teeth takes the box and walks around the back of the office building. I follow him a short distance, but not to the back of the building. The man with the long teeth doesn't come back. I wait awhile for him, then I feel silly for waiting at all when my business is done, so I go.

I'm home. I watch the Reds game. I get a call about the refrigerator. They might come over later, they don't know. They said they really wanted a side-by-side, not an over-under. I make some supper:

Freezer Queen macaroni and cheese, some potato chips, a beer. The beer is good.

Trudy comes home, goes into the kitchen and slides the backpack slowly down her arm. It hits the floor and slumps to one side.

"How was the meeting?" I say.

Trudy declares: "I'm exhausted."

Trudy opens and closes the cupboards. Dishes rattle. She comes over to me with a pile of eating utensils balanced precariously in her hammocked arms.

"God, I'm starved," she says, "—oh, the meeting? It went great! We got rid of all those NIMBY pamphlets—and Norma—*Norma!*—she got to talk with the Director of the State EPA—the *Director!*"

"That's pretty good, huh."

"Yeah. . . . Norma says he's a really nice guy. She says he's a good listener. She thinks he can really help us."

"Okay, fine, great," I say, "—here's another one in the paper—the *Tale of the Blowing Curtain*: You want to hear it?"

"Why not?" Trudy says. Her teeth are clenched. Her hands are in fists. But there's no turning back. I have to see this through.

> *The curtain in my kitchen was always blowing strongly because of a breeze from the window. So I took the bottom hem halfway out and slid a small metal chain through it and attached it at both ends of the curtain. After the chain was in place, I resewed the hem. The flexibility and weight of the chain adapts well to the need. Now the curtain stays put, and it was an easy task!*
> —*Dana B, Conway, New Hampshire.*

Trudy is silent a long time. I know that silence. I must have really zinged her with this one.

"So," Trudy says. "How was your day?"

"I took the stuff in the garage over to the recycle station."

"Fine, great, terrific," Trudy says and she goes upstairs.

I hear the shower going, then it's off. I have another beer, then I lock the doors and follow her up.

I'm in bed waiting for Trudy. When she comes into the bedroom, she wears her nightie, polyester made to look like silk, the one I bought her last Christmas for hot, romantic nights like this one. She comes around to her side of the bed, pulls back the covers and watches me watching her.

"What?" she asks me, sounding impatient that I am looking at her.

"Are you coming to bed? I mean are you going to sleep now?"

"No—I'm getting ready to ride the Kentucky Derby—and I know what you're thinking."

"No, you don't."

Trudy says: "It's too hot, forget it."

"It's not *that* at all. . . . I was just wondering."

"What."

"Who made you."

Trudy sighs, sits on the bed, swings her legs onto it, then pushes them under the covers. She is thinking a moment, then she flings the covers off her legs.

"Why don't you use that fucking newspaper to find a job."

"Just answer the question," I tell her.

"God made me, for Christ's sake."

She still sounds impatient; her voice is dutiful, brusque. But I can't resist.

". . . and Who is God?"

Trudy rolls onto her side, facing away. She squares her back to me.

"God is the maker of Heaven and Earth," she whispers sleepily.

"If God made Heaven and Earth, then who made Hell?"

Trudy is silent a long while. So, I go away and brush my teeth to kill time. When I come back, Trudy says: "You're not supposed to ask me *that*—nobody ever asked me *that* before."

"Why not?"

A breeze stiffens against the curtains in our bedroom, then the curtains are pushed far into the room by the air. Folds collapse into themselves and slap against the sill. Trudy is silent, silent in the way I've known other people to be silent, people who know things, but were never taught them, or people who were taught things, but who are never asked to say those things aloud.

I kill the light. I tell her, "I was just thinking that we might get some rain tonight."

"You think so?"

"God willing."

"Yeah, God willing."

"Maybe tomorrow I'll fix these curtains like it says in the *Enterprise*. I got a call about the refrigerator. Maybe I should try out *The Ice Cube Trick* before I get rid of it, huh?"

Trudy pulls a pillow to her chest. She stores it close to her body, and holds it tightly with both arms.

"Get outta here," she says.

The air outside the window begins to grope its way into the room. It is not cool air, only different from hot. It proceeds in strange waves of motion, almost imperceptible to the skin. Then there it is. Air. Cooler air. You have to kind of guess by the insubstantial way the air caresses you that it exists at all. Now the whole room is cooler; the air pulses in slightly more enduring waves. I hear a train go over the crossing in the center of town, the horn, the rhythmic clacking on the tracks, then thunder, the diesel. I hear the ensemble of sounds wane. A dog begins to bark. But there is something else, something almost indescribable, since its presence is not discrete. It is nearly unobtrusive, suggestive, like the bouquet of a wine, but more the part that is the subtle fragrance of fermentation. My garbage. Their garbage. Our garbage. Garbage— an odor that becomes on cool nights the refrain of a sad song, or a memory of one, a bad memory you want to block.

I say something to Trudy, something out loud, something maybe she hears, maybe not. I think how easy it is to speak nonsense when you think someone is asleep.

"I never expected you to answer that one about Hell," I tell her.

MARY MAGDALENA VERSUS GODZILLA

My sister Mary was always a bit unstable. Not mentally. I mean that even as a child she had the slightest tremor in her hands, not a shaking really, but something tremulous, the intimation of a quiver, the slightest shiver. I put her tremor down to her being born nearly two months early, incubated, and the result was her tremor and that she was stunted, "petite," she'd tell me later when she found a word that better suited her. "More like shrimpy," I'd tell her, but I'd be thinking "stunted."

But above all, Mary was easy, and I loved her for it, though I do not suggest she was easy in the way of sex, but easy to scare, frighten, easy to shock with even the most wildly fictitious events. When we were younger, I could convince her of anything, to a degree that satisfied me: something was after her, something enormous and terrifying, chasing her, just at her heels—something that would never relent. And in my mind Mary's unrelenting pursuer was Godzilla, that enormous prehistoric shadow in the feeble 1960 electric light of our television who wasted whole cities, and marched into Mary's mind and unformed fears.

And I was determined to make Mary's fears real. So when we were children, when she was about six and I was about nine, I'd tell her, "Godzilla can go anywhere. He came out of the deep Pacific after an H-Bomb test fractured the floor of the ocean. He came out of the sea into Tokyo Bay and lay waste to the city. Nothing can harm him . . . because he's radioactive, see?" Mary's small dark eyes would grow wide and I would feed on her eyes, elaborating, "He can just as easily come through the Panama Canal into the Atlantic Ocean, then up the Saint Lawrence Seaway, into Lake Erie—and he can destroy Cleveland. He can smash a house with one scaly foot; he can rip the side out of your bedroom with one toenail, or he can burn it off with the lasers in his eyes; he can take you in his claws and—CHOMP—like a Midgee Tootsie Roll . . . ."

I could tell my monstering got to her because she'd not say anything; she stood there listening to my story, sometimes with her thumb and two or three other fingers in her mouth, a bad habit she didn't break for years because I believe she stuck the fingers there to quell the tremor in her hand. It was clear to me from these primal gestures Mary never had the detached kind of scientific curiosity I had about the Big Guy, the Beast, Old Greenie, and other names movie hosts would at times call him, intimate names by which I came to know him. And a little after I'd finish my monstering, Mary'd grab her little red blanket and run from her room, for I made it a habit of pursuing her even there to relate my stories of the world's demise. Sometimes she'd run from her room directly into my room and lock the door.

Once Mother, frantic, had to wait half a day for Mary to come out. Another time, when Father had just come home from work, he had to remove the doorknob and mechanism to release her. But she never said why she locked the door. I escaped unscathed each time I drove her into my room in fear. And I believe her silence, her not squealing on me, as it were, had something to do with fear itself—and something less obvious, something connected, I felt, to her congenital conditions, her tremor and being stunted, or as she put it, "petite": because of her condition no one seemed to expect her to explain herself.

And in a way I believe it was also her silence, her unobtrusive ways, that made me continue to pursue her. I caught her the next day after Father had released her from my room, sitting in the kitchen, peeling the crust off a slice of white bread, something that annoyed me to no end, something bird-like, her way of pinching the crust with her twiggy little fingers and tearing it off a little strip at a time, then pecking out the white center with her tiny lips. It was no way to eat, just the center of a slice of bread all by itself—no sandwich, no meat, no mayonnaise, no nothing. So I intervened. I said, "Come out back with me. I want to show you something."

I grabbed her by the arm and tugged her out the back door. She followed, hanging onto the mutilated slice of bread all the while. When we got to the driveway near the garage door, I said, "You see those power lines over there?"

Mary didn't talk. It was her way. She pecked at her bread and nodded slightly, her eyes on me in a half-distracted stare, trying to look at me and the power lines at the same time. Then she moved her head, ever so slightly along the path the power lines cut, pole to pole.

"Well, do you see them?" I said.

She nodded.

"Godzilla can tear right through them like Mom's laundry line." I pointed at Mother's line, flying all our clothes in the summer wind like flags. "He can tear those lines down and knock the poles over. Electricity can't stop him. *Nothing* can stop him." I ran to the center of our back yard and made long, slow monster steps toward Mary's bedroom window, and added, "He'll walk right up to your room and rip the wall open." I made a gesture, clawing at the green wooden siding of our house. "Then he'll burn you alive with his fire breath." I opened my mouth and hissed, forcing as much air as I could through my partially restricted epiglottis to make a sound as close to fire breathing as I could, and when I turned to look, Mary had gone. . . .

Later that night, Mary knocked at my bedroom door. I could tell it was her. The tapping was feeble, but syncopated, fast, and desperate. I opened my door a crack, just enough to see one dark eye of hers and one lock of her black hair, like a wing, partially covering the eye.

"What," I said.

She stood looking at me until I saw the eye glisten slightly with moisture.

"Okay," I whispered and let her in.

She had her red blanket with her, held tightly against her nightie and chest, like a shield. After I shut the door and got back into bed, I watched her turn her back to me, make a secretive gesture with her hands, and let the red blanket slip to the floor at her feet. She dragged a corner of the blanket with one toe, then used a toe of her other foot to square it as best she could. For a time she knelt on it, then she lay on it and slept, my premature sister, in one corner of my room, as if she had never been removed from her incubator after birth.

When I woke, the sun was barely up, and a line of light from the window where the shade did not quite meet the sill cut across her small, curled form in the corner. I got up and nudged her with my foot.

"Come on," I said. "Get out of here before Mom comes."

If monstering Mary was one of my early successes in life, one of the greatest disappointments was that I never went away to a presti-gious college like many of my high school friends, big schools with stately names such as THE OHIO STATE UNIVERSITY, the great center of agricultural engineering, or small, little-known schools founded on lofty principles, or faraway schools, ones that I thought would be a sea change for me into something strange and fantastic, such as the INCARNATE WORD COLLEGE in San Antonio, Texas, "a Catholic co-educational college," the brochure said, "of liberal arts and professional studies with a social justice orientation." My one and only girlfriend, Martha, gave me the brochure, planned on attending herself, and after one semester at INCARNATE WORD returned to Cleveland, singing the funniest little song:

> The other night, friend,
> as I lay sleeping . . .
> I dreamed we had no Catholic Press
> and when I awoke it was not so,
> and I had some sunshine today!

Despite my obvious disillusionment with INCARNATE WORD, I still wanted to attend just to be with Martha, but could not afford the out-of-state tuition. Her next visit home, Martha dumped me for a theology major.

So I spent two years at Cuyahoga Community College, the Western Campus, a converted army barracks, then finished a major in business at Cleveland State. Still, despite being a townie all those years, I can't say that the experience led to utter despair. I had Mary. Although she had grown a foot taller, she continued to fascinate me with her silent, timid ways, and for a time when she was finishing high school she became rather a challenge. Sure, I still believed that she harbored secret fears of Old Greenie, of death by being eaten, burned, or squashed, yet I'll admit, she was different. I won't say Mary, nearly seventeen, had grown cynical in her old age, but she had grown, shall I say, less susceptible to direct terrorism. I concluded this was partly because of her numerous boyfriends, breaking up with one, taking up with another. . . . The pattern was predictable and I theorized that predictability led to a kind of cynicism. Besides, I was a little envious that Mary went through boyfriends like pairs of socks and I'd been traded in for a theology major.

So I had to make even more elaborate productions to elicit even the vaguest signs of terror from Mary. In her case, being nearly seventeen, this response was laughter. So laughter became the standard of the day, the substitute for the terrors of the decade before, those frightening 60's—and why not? Was the kind of terrorizing I perpetrated on my sister, her laughter masking her fear, far different than what I then watched on television, what my entire family watched? Surely a sitcom like *My Mother the Car*, a man's dear mother returning from the dead as some sort of Model T, was terrifying. We could scream and laugh out two sides of our consciousnesses, never thinking that the logical end for the mother in the series was the junkyard.

Besides, there were vestiges of the old days of my monstering of Mary. She still had the tremor in her hands, something the doctors at last concluded was congenital, would only worsen, and which caused her to pocket them or to hold them together behind her back to keep them from trembling.

So nearing my graduation from Cleveland State, feeling a little trepidation that I would soon be *out there* on my own, as it were, and knowing my sister had been the best audience for my monstering I had ever known, I conceived of a plan I could put my heart into, something that would no doubt send my borderline cynical, yet still rather innocent sister into fits of laughter—and terror.

Late one night, about two a.m., when I was sure Mary was asleep, I got out of bed, went to my closet, took my recent purchase from the top shelf, and unwrapped it. In the box was a Godzilla head I'd gotten through the mail for thirty bucks from Movie Publishers Incorporated in Canoga Park, California. It was a fair likeness of the Big Guy himself: his red eyes were set deep in his scaly green reptilian skull, eyes that seemed to reflect anger, disappointment—and something else. Being almost a college graduate, and having expanded my knowledge of the world, I made a short mental analysis of Godzilla's subtle countenance and concluded that it reminded me of a kind of compassionate stoicism, with only lapses into the unbridled rage for which he was known. This led me into a series of scholarly speculations since I had been thinking lately of going to graduate school at Cleveland State to major in—who knows?—wanting only to continue my deferment from the draft, anything but business—and Vietnam. So these speculations took the form of short topics for discourse on Zap Breath: "Godzilla's Stoicism," "An Etymological Note on *Godzilla*," "Godzilla and the Incas," "Godzilla and the Critics," after J.R.R. Tolkien's famous 1936 address, "The Monsters and the Critics," and more. . . .

But I shook off such musings, noting as I sized up my monster head, how nicely the teeth looked. The top fangs were long and hard and colored a disgusting brownish yellow, and the remaining slashers were even more tarnished with what I speculated was dried human blood. The slashers were sharp like needles, and all ran together at odd angles, like parts of a vicious trap I'd seen on a newscast of Vietnam—a horrible way to kill an unsuspecting soldier. He'd fall into a pit of sharpened wooden stakes at all angles, sometimes smeared with human feces just in case death was not immediate . . . but I was straying from my task! What did Vietnam have to do with Godzilla anyway?

So I again shook off these distractions, slipped the Godzilla head over my own, and I was in full persona, the height of my abilities, feeling the hard plastic over my ears, my hot breath rising up and out the nostril holes in the mask. It was early summer, so I began to sweat inside the mask, and a bit of it came down my brow and ran into my eyes. I blinked in my eye holes just below Godzilla's. My eyes stung inside his eyes—and I knew it was time. . . . Our parents were out of town. It was perfect.

Godzilla goes down the hall, Creak, Creak, *stops at unsuspecting woman's bedroom door,* Thunk. *He bursts into her room, shrieking with primeval anguish, his reptilian howl*—ARGHIAAH!— ARGHIAAH! Thud, Thud. . . . *Godzilla sees Todd Kramer, Mary's boyfriend, humping her, his hairy buttocks swinging up and down, and Mary's little premature legs on each side of the gargantuan buttocks, pulling back and thrusting themselves out.* Thunk. *He smells a sweet, pungent odor in his scaly nostrils, but it is not the sulfurous scent of smoldering Tokyo—it is* Cannabis. . . . *Godzilla sees their terrified faces, Todd Kramer slip out of the open window holding his pants in his hands; and Mary says to the green hulking beast, clutching her bed sheets to her chest:*

"What's the matter with you? Why don't you just destroy Cleveland or something—like any self-respecting monster? Damn you! Get out of here!"

. . . and so Godzilla, shaken to the core of his cold-blooded heart, retreats to his room. . . . Then, later that morning, about three a.m., he hears a feeble rap at his door . . . and in comes Mary the fallen woman. She carries her sleeping bag under one arm. Her hands tremble. She unrolls the bag and lays it in a corner of the room. Godzilla sees her small red baby blanket tucked inside the flap of the bag. Mary looks at Godzilla and makes a little laugh. She sleeps in his room, curled into one corner.

The next month after my monstering of Mary and Todd, the day after Mary graduated from high school, she ran off with Todd Kramer.

She married him and they found an apartment in a suburb of Akron, Goodyear Heights.

I never attended graduate school. Nixon—someone—ended the draft, a great *deus ex machina* for hold-outs like me whose student deferments had become low lottery numbers . . . a sea change. . . . So I went to work in Downtown Cleveland at a smelter off Euclid Avenue, Mosca Industries, where they re-refined what were to some industries precious metals: cadmium, magnesium, tungsten, and the like. The smelter was smoky and smelled oily and metallic, and reminded me of Godzilla's urban ruin and destruction most of the time.

Goodyear Heights wasn't all that far away from Cleveland. I figured Uncle Thunder Breath could visit the little woman, her hubby, and as time went on their four children. On one visit, when I described my work at Mosca Industries to Mary, she seemed repulsed, not like I'd ever seen her before. She seemed as terrified of my work as she had of Godzilla when we were kids. Perhaps more.

"You poor thing," she said.

I became angry. I didn't need her pity—me! I told her that at least I finished college and had a job, and she turned and walked away, silent, holding her hands in front of her, away from my eyes.

So for a time things were shaky between Mary and me. But I still had my diversion. Little Mary and her family moved to a small house in Goodyear Heights and became part of Godzilla's Great Chain of Being. There was a whole new generation to monster. So I donned my toothy Godzilla head and terrorized her kids with good results, even when they were older and learned to replace terror with laughter.

But as the years passed, Mary changed. Even when I was only visiting, I'd find her sitting in her kitchen staring blankly at a wall. All the appliances would be unplugged. The black cords hung limply from the edges of the counters. The sink was full of dishes, and when she'd make a feeble effort to wash them, she did so by hand, despite having an automatic dishwasher. She seemed a little like an amoeba in a jet-age kitchen, slow, floating, out of place. She grew haggard and puffy in her face. Her skin, which at one time had been the color of porcelain—

not actually looking healthy, but still smooth, white, and appealing—had now grown ruddy and splotchy. Even my best Godzilla shows during my more and more frequent visits failed to cheer her. One visit during Thanksgiving I even constructed a miniature of the Goodyear Rubber Plant, and Godzilla destroyed it in her living room during a Browns football game. I stood there in my Godzilla head in the middle of her living room amid the rubble of the rubber factory, her kids cheering around me, and waited for her to smile, smirk, fold her arms in parental indignation . . . anything. But even in the aftermath of the wanton and complete destruction of Goodyear, she looked detached, distant.

Just before Christmas that same year, Mother told me that Mary had run off to New York City without Todd or her kids. I worked on this new development in my mind several months, thinking, what would the Big Guy do? So, in the tradition of Old Greenie, without announcing myself, I flew to New York and took a room at the Washington Square Hotel. I looked her up in the directory and called her number in the East Village. Imagine it. She seemed happy to hear from me.

"You! Big Guy!" she said. "Wonderful—lovely—perfect—love to see you!—let's meet at the Metropolitan Museum about, say, twoish?"

I didn't doubt for a moment that the voice on the phone was my sister's: Mary, Mary the Timid, Mary the Fallen, Mary the Small and Curled Form on My Bedroom Floor, Mother Mary, Work Weary Mary of the Four Children and Todd—it was plainly her voice. But she'd never used the words *wonderful* or *lovely* the whole time I'd known her, and *twoish* didn't exist on the faces of clocks in Cleveland—or Goodyear Heights. . . . I vaguely feared that someone had broken into her apartment because I heard a male voice—perhaps two—prattling softly in the background in the receiver. I figured someone was forcing her to talk to me that phony way so I wouldn't get wise that she was being held against her will.

It was nearly one anyway, so my plan was to try to meet her at the museum. If she didn't show, then I'd go to the East Village, beat her door in and lay waste to the felons, *wonderful, lovely, perfect*, a great opportunity to play the Big Guy, the Incarnation of Justice, as it were.

So I was a bit surprised when I saw Mary in the Great Hall of the Museum leaning on a Doric column. A tattered red velvet beret sat atop her tiny head, cocked down, concealing one eye. Her black hair was cropped to boyish length and she wore tight black vinyl pants, a bad approximation of leather. Her sweat shirt was ripped, revealing her shoulders and most of her upper chest, nearly to the ends of her tiny, barely distinct breasts. Several great orange hoops ran through the lobes of her ears. They clanked together when she noticed me and turned slightly to look at me, her cigarette hanging from her lip, not as if she were smoking it, but as though it were another kind of accessory, an ashy, smoking piece of her outfit. At first, I had to resist the impression that she was not *my* sister, but then I saw that she'd gotten her porcelain complexion back; she still looked a bit haggard, but the ruddiness had gone from her face. She seemed in that small respect her old self.

"Hi," she said in a tone of voice more like the one I remembered, more like Premature Mary than Neo-Beat Mary. She stabbed her cigarette into the sand of a great Persian vase, then turned to me, sprung to her tiptoes, took me by both shoulders and kissed me lightly on one cheek then the other. She turned and went straight to the staircase. I followed her, and she was quiet a long time as we made the stairs to the Medieval Room, then she said, not looking at me, but turning to a reliquary box in the exhibit.

"You don't have to ask. I'll tell you. I'm an art history student at NYU. . . . There's nothing more to it." Then she pointed at another reliquary object. "This one contains a small vial of water and in it a tooth, presumably one of Mary Magdalena's. Isn't it marvelous?"

I didn't know what was so marvelous about the tooth. It looked like a specimen of a pituitary gland in formaldehyde I'd seen once in Dr. Whitaker's office in Cleveland. I leaned in to read the plaque: RELIQUARY TOOTH OF MARY MAGDALENA, FLORENCE, 15TH CENTURY. I couldn't believe that anyone could be so dumb to believe the tooth was the real thing, and somehow even the modifier, "reliquary," didn't hold water or make a good enough excuse for believing it, so I said, "So, Mary, looks like you've lost an incisor there."

I wanted my remark to get a laugh, needed it really, but she stood there, looking brutally Beat, as if she hadn't a clue to what I'd meant, so I conjured all my primeval power, looked to the Great Source of my life's endeavor and inspiration—I had to get control of the situation—and said to her, "Yeah, right, I get it . . . *Reliquary Tooth of Godzilla, Florence, Fifteenth Century.*"

I waited for a laugh, wince, embarrassed tick in the face, any sign from her, but she simply turned and walked on, straight for another object, a silver dove suspended over an altarpiece. . . . I couldn't give up, felt I may have tapped a vein of fear by her indifferent reaction. I thought,

Perhaps . . .

Then she pointed at the silver dove and said, "This is exquisite. Don't you think?"

I replied, "Yes, exquisite, *Eucharistic Godzilla Above Altarpiece.*"

I could see she was breaking down: she glanced around the exhibit to see if anyone had heard me. Her hands that she so habitually kept at her sides or held together in front of her, began to tremble and she nervously wrung them. Finally, she fled at a brisk pace to another exhibit, European Paintings. And I pursued her:

"Poussin," she whispered, her voice becoming soft and uncertain.

"Yes," I said, *"Blind Godzilla Searching for the Rising Sun,* 1658."

Then I followed her to the Twentieth-Century Wing.

"Kandinsky," she muttered as her dark eyes glanced from the work on the wall to the other people viewing the exhibits.

"Wonderful," I added, *"The Garden of Godzilla: Improvisation Number Twenty-Two,* 1949. . . . Right?"

And, "These two . . . Klee. . . ."

"So *true,*" I said in a nasal, breathy voice, *"The Pathos of Godzilla,* 1921 . . . and, oh yes, of course! *The Chair Godzilla,* 1922!"

My pursuit of her was not easy—my Mary Magdalena could never be angry, had always chosen silence or flight, and I must admit, even for a guy with thick skin like me, it was hard to keep on with it, so I stopped taunting her, but it was too late; near the Ancient China Wing, in the voice I had always known her to have, Mary, my Mary Magdalena, finally her old self, said, "Look, I know what you're doing, but you don't have to anymore. I know you're just trying to cheer me up, but you don't have to, really. . . . You suffer, you go through hell, then the time comes to be happy . . . so I'm happy, all right?"

She kissed me again on each cheek and left me there, in Ancient China, feeling like a failure, like my monstering days had come to an end.

Later that night, I got a bite to eat at the Pink Tearoom, a concoction of pasta, butter, and scallions, but I longed to have something I could get my teeth into. I wanted to go home. So rather dejected, I walked aimlessly around Washington Square, pausing under the great arch, wanting to tear it down, but feeling very small, thinking, yeah, that would be a piece of cake for the Big Guy, but for *me*? The sun set and I went to my room at the hotel. Very late, I don't know what time, I heard a knock at my door, asked who it was, and let in Mary Magdalena. She removed the surplus army coat she was wearing, spread her red blanket across the seat of the easy chair and slept. She was stoned, very stoned, and though I wanted to talk, to shake her from sleep, to ask her if she thought I was a genuine failure, I was tired, very tired. . . .

Over the next five years, Mary Magdalena and I exchanged letters. I wrote to her about the specialty metals business, to which she never failed to respond, *I'm sorry*, or *Poor thing*. I mentioned in my letters new movies I'd seen, including, of course, some of the new greats comprising the Godzilla canon, *Destroy All Monsters*, *Godzilla Versus the Cosmic Monster* and, of course, a title that raised her curiosity, *The Terror of Mechagodzilla*. Mary wrote that she changed majors at NYU . . . from art history to art to social work to dance to political science to journalism to pre-law to poetry writing . . . philosophy . . .

playwriting. . . . She'd stayed with play writing a whole year, so I fed off that, sending her bits of my vast knowledge of the subject, what I'd heard was happening in theater, say, Off-Broadway, productions such as, *Godzilla! A Day in the Life* and *Godzilla. Now It Can be Told*, and a cabaret piece, *The Fabulous Godzilla Show!* And on Broadway, *Dial M. for Monster* and the seminal production, *Godzilla!* I wrote to her in a religious tone, "Take these and use them. They are good ideas—right for our times." But she replied, "I want to write a great drama, something enduring, a brave myth." And in a later letter she seemed exasperated by my penchant for the Big Guy and reminded me that her pursuit of dramaturgy was serious. Of course, I complied with her demand for higher artistic purpose, responding with Godzilla's *Glass Menagerie*, a masterwork, I wrote, "full of deep psychological insights into the monster and his interest in expressionism." I also felt I could particularly interest her in the author's representation of his sister in the work, but Mary didn't respond to my letter at all.

And she never mentioned Todd or her children.

The next I heard from Mary, she was in Japan, a card from Hiroshima, on which she briefly described her participation in the lighting of candles in little paper boats and floating them out to sea to commemorate the victims of the atomic blast there in 1945. Her handwriting was shaky, nearly illegible. But she ended her card by saying she had been so moved by the ceremony that she had tossed her red baby blanket into the ocean.

Of course that island, Japan, had been Godzilla's old stomping ground, so I was interested in the card. But after Hiroshima a year passed. I didn't hear from her at all. Sensing that she was so far away, seeming to get farther each year, I suddenly felt it was time to dust off the Godzilla head and take it to New York, where Mother had gotten a recent address for her.

I could have called ahead, but it was not my way. Besides, Mother had been very sure about the address in the West Village, less sure about the telephone number since no one had answered on several occasions when she'd called it. So, knowing the dangers of unannounced visits, I packed the Godzilla head in my gym bag and made off again for New York. The address was on Christopher Street, a quiet place, where suddenly the village walkers disappeared and a calm surrounded me, not in a creepy way, just a lonely, isolated way. The deserted street, seeing the steps coming down from the apartment buildings with no one sitting on them, reminded me of *Five*, a classic science fiction flick . . . only five people are left after the atomic holocaust. . . .

I stopped near Mary's apartment, set my gym bag down, unzipped it, and removed my Godzilla head, thinking how embarrassing it had been the last time I'd tried this, but how Mary and I had come so far in life. I was sure she'd understand. So I slipped on the head and proceeded to her apartment. . . .

Godzilla sees the apartment building, Thud, Thud, *steps into a bag of garbage ripped open and spilling into the street,* Crunch, Crunch. *He sees the stairs to the apartment and climbs them,* Thunk, Thunk, Thunk. *He sees her front door.* Clunk. *He stops and tries the doorknob,* Creak, Creak, *finds it open.* Thud. *Godzilla looks right, looks left.* Thud. *He sees a door, white enamel, wood showing through it where the paint is peeled away.* Thunk. *He crashes through the door.* ARGHIAAH! . . . ARGHIAAH! Thud, Thud. *Godzilla sees animal shit on the floor and chairs overturned . . . dishes broken and flies swarming over food on the counter and floors. His great heart pauses. . . . He sees Mary slouched back in a chair at a small white table.* Thunk. *He goes to her.* Thud, Thud. *He sees her eyes, no longer dark and shiny, but milky and blank, two pale stones.* Thud. *Her hands dangle from her sides, no longer trembling. He reaches for her.* Creak. *He touches her pale face with a scaly claw.* Creak. *No response.* Thud. *The Great Reptile thinks, 'What has laid waste to this world? Could the creature before me, this tiny premature being, have possessed the inestimable power to cause such wreckage?' Godzilla backs away in confusion.* Thunk, Thunk.

'A power greater than his?' Thud. *He moves forward,* Creak. *His great head turns a little left, a little right . . . and Mary suddenly*

moves. . . . Godzilla jumps. Thud.

"You again," Mary mumbles and rolls her milky eyes in her head. "What the fuck do you want now? Leave me alone. Let me BE!"*Godzilla backs away.* Creak, Creak. *His great Godzilla chin falls to his chest,* Thud. *Angry and bewildered, he shrieks*, ARGHIAAH! *then, resigned,* ARGhiaah . . . arghiaah. . . .

I sat a short while on the steps outside her apartment with my Godzilla head in my lap, then went inside to discover she had gone out the back way. I wondered: had Mary Magdalena defeated Godzilla? Had she with cold white eye and brave numbness of spirit struck dumb even the most dreadful monster of all? Would he no longer lumber into town, vent his primeval reptilian anguish, no longer care about the screaming throngs of people he pursues through the streets of the City—or the laughter behind their terror? Had she sent him back, alone, to his watery grave? . . . And now, now, must I, whatever I am, emerge to redeem my premature trembling sister? But will my footfalls be hollow, my empty howl unheard in a land where monstering no longer matters?

When I returned to sit on the steps outside her apartment, several people were strolling along Christopher Street—*amazing*, I thought—*people.* I'd been so sure I'd flattened them all—done the job, complete. From my steps I watched these people for a long time—that is how I first took to studying hands and faces, the ways people conceal hands from view, the slightest tremors in their fingers, and the cold white ache of faces drawn and silent.

Some days, through my single eyeholes I see the smallest signs of their terror everywhere, other days, nowhere, and without Mary I find I need to depend entirely upon my imagination. It is days such as these, when nothing is as it seems, when I believe I might have made my monstering better, days in my sleep in my watery catacombs, when Godzilla emerges from the great depths of the ocean, comes into the Saint Lawrence, into Lake Erie, finds our old house in Cleveland, tears the back off it, and sees little Mary in her room . . . but she is no longer afraid of him. She is changed. She does not tremble or stare at him with her tiny dark eyes and speechless expression. She stands squarely over her red blanket, two fists at her sides. She is Magdalena, the image frozen in his great reptilian eye . . . and he takes her into his scaly arms. He lets nothing stop him until he finds the open sea again. He walks into the sea with her—and deep in the ocean, even in the darkest part of the Pacific, Godzilla sees the place of his origin, the place he had slept millennia before an H-Bomb cracked the ocean's floor, shook the world, and roused the angry monster from his slumber. There, he carries his sister with him, back, back into that sleep, back, before the time of monsters when all things were possible.

II. From the Wall

The din was renewed, the noise redoubled;
    Each man of the Danes was mute with dread,
    That heard from the wall the terrible wail
      The gruesome song. . . .

        —Beowulf (1000 A.D.?),
        translation by J. Duncan Spaeth

GOING LONG

Ta-ra-ra boom-de-ay, sit on the curb I may . . .
—Chekhov, *The Three Sisters*

You should see this guy, I tell my wife. See how he holds the ball, how he backs away from center, bounds back on his heels, *his heels mind you*, throws off balance, like there's no tomorrow, like he's got to throw the ball now or never. Some other guy's coming at him like a bullet, like he's at the speed of sound, but it only looks that way since he shoots out from the edge of the TV screen like a cannonball, headed right for this quarterback, Number 8. This guy shooting out from the edge of the screen, he's like a dead guy with his arms stretched out, like some ghoul in *The Night of the Living Dead*, except he's going faster, a lot faster, going right for Number 8. And this Number 8, he isn't even looking downfield half the time; I swear he's even got his eyes closed when he lets the ball fly; then it's snagged by this other guy going deep.

Now, that's communication, I tell my wife, and I ask her to bring me more diet spiced cider. *I mean*, I say, *now that's the ultimate in making contact with another human being.* That ball, it crosses all that

empty space, that crazy, loud, crying collage-like crowd blurred behind it, with only one intent: reaching that other guy, coming in right
on his numbers. One guy's getting creamed and he doesn't even know
if the next guy, acres down the field, will even get the message. I mean,
this guy throwing the ball, he just has this weird kind of faith, just like
that other guy, gliding underneath it, to a spot where he was always
meant to be, like Father Time put it in his appointment book.

It's like if guys like him never caught the balls they were supposed
to, or caught the ones they had dropped, our whole history might be
changed. Guys like Hitler would have never been anyone; there might
have been worse, or maybe better. Shoot, maybe plastics would have
never been invented, or man-made shoes like my father made me wear.
Weird stuff. But you have to believe. You have to feel a little like
there's something to it. That catch, Number 8 flat on his back, and the
other guy, way downfield, getting the message, careening off these
other guys trying to flatten him—it was like a kind of faith, like a kind
of order I had never seen before. Though I'd seen football before.
Though I have indulged in it socially. Though I am not a heavy fan.
Though I can't recall watching the game by myself, like now. But it
was predestination at work, in living color, the feathers of a graphical
peacock, the network logo, evoking exactly what it should. What you
saw was what you got for tuning in. But it didn't look like anything at
all—they always say athletes make it look so easy, and I believe it,
especially on the tube.

Christ, what a throw. What a catch. *Hey,* I call into the kitchen to
my wife, *they're carrying Number 8 off the field—now they've got him
up, honey, and two guys are helping him walk. Where's my cider?*

Now this is halftime; I mean Number 8 got creamed right before
halftime, just after a big gain, which didn't matter because the clock
ran out. This Number 8, he didn't have a real good passing average in

the first half—IT FLASHES ON THE SCREEN—*38 %* complete. I
suppose that isn't very good. His team doesn't have any points. *I suppose*, I tell my wife who settles beside me with my hot diet cider, *he
should be grateful.* The other team doesn't have any points, either.
Mack, my wife says, *you're going to vitrify in front of the TV.* That's
the best she can come up with. VITRIFY! What kind of word is that?
Vitrify, my ass.

A little ways into halftime, I'm beginning to aggravate my wife. I
mean I'm starting the one thing she hates most; but before I start going
into my various philosophies of life, I explain to her that the reason
I'm playing with her mind is because nobody warned me that halftime
could be so boring: a couple of sportscasters on the tube are sitting
behind this panel, or news counter, or whatever it is—IS THERE A
REAL WORD FOR THIS THING THEY'RE SITTING BEHIND?
Anyway, they're going on about this quarterback, this Number 8, and
his lousy percentage; I mean they're citing his averages last game, last
year, his last team before they traded him, his whole career, his life
before, his afterlife. . . . I mean I didn't go into the whole thing with my
wife. I just sipped on the cider and said this *halftime* is BORING, very
dull stuff—and that got it to her, my own brand of the long one
downfield: *boring* I mumbled, and she knew, like she always knows,
just like the guy going deep. He knows which way to break. Sometimes she knows just how to react to my words. It's uncanny, like she's
got eyes on the top of her head same as that guy going for the pass—
radar—scoping in on the meaning coming at her—boring, the ball—
God I love my wife sometimes: great hands, I think.

What I was trying to get at is my philosophy, which I have tried on
a lot of guys in a lot of states of mind: some of them get it, some of
them say they do, but they don't. Some of them—the really honest, or
straight, or sober guys—say what I'm telling them doesn't make a
goddamned bit of sense. So I try my philosophies out on my wife, and
she says the same thing as the honest and sober guys, but the way she
says it is different. And I don't know if I can really explain it—it's like

this Mother Mary smile breaks over her face, the same kind of smile she used to get when I'd get my ass chewed by her old man for bringing her home late (then I'd get my ass chewed again by *my* old man for being so long getting my ass chewed by *her* old man). But that's not the point! It's more like her mouth, the sounds coming out, are put there by something else, like she knows she has to say my philosophy is bullshit, and the smile is another part of her speaking, saying something like *Mister Mackerel, Mister Mackerel, I got what you're trying to say, I really got it, but I can't tell you I got it in any way you'd understand, so just watch me smile about it, and shut up for Christ's sake!*

SO . . . I'm trying it again anyway, I'm telling her my global, holistic, all-encompassing, life-long contemplated, beyond the grave, before and after the advent of the automobile, philosophy. She's saying, *Mister Mack, the marching band isn't half bad; they're striking up 'When You Wish Upon a Star'.* . . . *I know, I know,* I say, but how can anyone anymore wish on one star? What's needed are new philosophies—the more the better!—and I want her to listen real good because I'm only going to say it once more. My philosophies of life go like this: most intelligent people can hold two opposing ideas in their heads at the same time, so I suppose that leaves out people of real faith. But it really doesn't leave out people with faith, because I know people of real faith, people who trust in one thing, tease it out their whole lives, string it out and go over the thing they believe in again and again, and those people get a whole set of new things out of that faith, different kinds of personal power, like when money just naturally comes to some folks, and when all those new unexpected things come out of their faith—I DON'T KNOW WHAT KINDS OF THINGS—like peace of mind, or money like I said, or more children than they ever dreamed of, or good friends who would die for them, or all of the above. . . . But all these NEW things suddenly become opposites, and they think they have to choose between them, like do I want money OR peace of mind, or do I want living bad friends OR dead good ones? SO then these people of faith have to find a new faith and start all over, or they just have to hold these opposite things in their heads and think they're NOT NORMAL—and that, THAT is the clincher, the RUB, the ultimate thing of it all: they ARE NORMAL because everyone's all the time thinking, and holding these opposites in their heads, and getting faith, then getting it all over again so they don't have to choose anything else that came out of that original faith. It's like the BIG BANG always going on in our heads, like the universe shrinking into one particle the size of a pebble and weighing a zillion tons, then exploding into crazy quilt galaxies speckled with a gazillion stars, then shrinking and blowing out again, over and over.

Screw you if you can't take a joke, I tell my wife, which suddenly strikes me as making no sense since she's got that nutty smile on her face again. Did she really think they understood philosophers in the times in which they lived? HELL NO. Shit no; it's like making sloppy joes. I can always tell a sloppy joe that hasn't been simmered long enough to get all the flavors and juices to marry in the sauce; it takes time, same as things have to cook in people, especially people who have these philosophical forces going on in them and they don't even know it. It takes them time to know these things are steaming inside themselves, so long in fact that the philosophers die off, and then they get recognized—isn't that the way with most things? I mean look at what Norman Rockwell's stuff is going for these days. They don't believe you until you're dead. So if that's what you're smiling about, YOU ARE RIGHT, but you could be kinder about it, that's all. Maybe you could pretend I was dead, and pretend how you would feel after I was gone, and see if that feeling included realizing that my philosophy was right. Maybe sometime I'll write it down and give it to you so you can refer to it when I'm gone. *Jesus, put some rum in this cider next time,* I tell her. *After this halftime show, I'm going to need the libation.*

I ask my wife if she's going to stick around for the second half of the game. She tells me I'm not a fan, so why am I bothering? Do I want to run to the store with her? She needs some menstrual pads. I tell her no, I'll pass, you go along and have fun. She reaches up and pats her mouth—that smile—with her hand. She blows me a kiss, and I never get it, because I'm dying to know who's going to replace Number 8, who got flattened by the defensive lineman on that long pass downfield. *Okay*, she says, do I want anything? World peace I tell her, like I always tell her when I really don't want anything.

So we're coming to the incredible part: I mean I told you everything so far: how Number 8 got creamed, only he connected on that long pass, but how he didn't get any points because time ran out. I told you about my philosophies that no one can understand until I die, about my wife and her weird smiles, about my wife and her menstrual pads, about the libation my wife has prepared for me in the guise of spiced cider. I've told you about the ESSENCE OF COMMUNICATION, some pretty weird stuff that you can never understand since I'm still alive, and even if I ask you to imagine that I am dead and rethink what I've just said, you probably still won't get it because you will know I am alive (though I really believe you will try to imagine otherwise). Anyway, I wouldn't blame you if you tried. BUT THIS IS THE POINT, this is the absolutely mind-boggling thing about it:

NUMBER 8 IS IN THE GAME!

But he isn't really RIGHT, old Number 8. I mean he doesn't look real sure of himself, and there are all of these little bullet-shaped red marks on his pants on his thigh where he's reached up, wiped the blood from under his nose, reached down, and blotted the blood on his pants. Nonetheless, he's there after the kickoff, starting from his own 17-yard line, taking snap after snap and putting the ball up on every down; he's hitting his receivers left and right, picking them at the trailing end of buttonhooks, down and outs, crossing patterns. The guy seems infallible. He drills one in the end zone, and the announcers are going

nuts like you never hear them go nuts anymore, except maybe in the
Olympics when the USA takes medals that they're never supposed to
get. Eight for eight this guy is. WOW. Eight for eight for Number 8.

The other team can't do anything with the ball, so they punt it, and
Number 8 comes out again, dragging ass, in a torn jersey that hangs out,
more blood bullets down the sides of his pants, fresh tape on his ankles.
He's swaggering, but not like a man fresh for the battle; he's swaggering
like he's taking a final walk to glory; he's Sergeant York, like he's too
naive to know he's captured the whole blessed army; he's beat to hell,
but he's swaggering onto the field like a machine that's really broken-in.
Then he's taking snaps again, rolling to his left, popping receivers. A
screen play. A hand-off. Then a draw play that blows right by the middle
linebacker; now Number 8's RUNNING!—and holding the ball in both
arms, rocking it like a baby as he barrels through the defensive line. This
guy isn't for real, and the TV announcers are updating their statistics,
flashing up his rushing yards on the screen, minute-by-minute updates
of his percentage complete. They're forgetting altogether about this guy's
mediocre career, like he was born when he walked on the field in the
second half. Now he's TWELVE FOR TWELVE, and his pants look
like blood has rained on them, and it strikes me, it flat hits me between
the eyes: I can see everything I was talking to my wife about, everything
I've ever told to my friends, my father, my mother, the dog when no one
was around. Stuff about my philosophies. I begin to see the strangest
things about my life, right in the middle of Number 8's rain of blood
bullets, the way he sails the ball, gets murdered as he releases it, the way
it spirals, wobbling with the last perturbation of the blow he takes to the
head and stomach from the onrushing line, the way the ball still overcomes that queer aerodynamic flaw to find the receiver. Right when I
know this guy is operating on pure, 100%, unadulterated, skin of the
teeth, blind as a bat faith, right when I can follow the flight of the ball,
knowing even before it left his hand where it was bound, I can see everything about the earth—CRAZY STUFF—the mountains under the

oceans, all of the continental divides at the same time, watersheds spanning thousands of square miles in all places of the world at once, the cut of the imaginary rocks I am standing on, the rug of trees losing itself in a kind of infinity, a mist, a haze, no people.

I know, but I'm not really paying attention to it, that Number 8 is hitting EVERYTHING IN SIGHT. Another touchdown. He hits a guy over the middle by the goal posts at the back of the end zone. Later, he lofts a touch pass, like a feather, a gift to the receiver, a delicate, wonderful thing. AND I AM AMAZED, I AM DESOLATE, the way you're always the most alone when something amazing's happening and you're dying to have someone to be with you to see it happen, partly so that they will believe you, but partly for something else, something I can't say, only that I feel it, and I'm cursing my wife to get her ass home so she can believe this bloodied-up son of a bitch, and how he's cutting up this defense.

As I am watching this man loft the ball with such pain and ease at the same time, I can feel the roundness of the world, its relief in the palm of my hand, the wetness of its water as my skin presses over the waves of the ocean; now Number 8's slammed to the turf, and it seems like every irregularity, every grumble and groan in the earth's crust, every meteorological disturbance, every twister, typhoon, every forest fire, is in me to witness: there are more blood bullets on this man's pants now, and he's wiping his forehead, has his hands on his knees a moment before he steps up to the line to take the next snap, and I'm thinking JESUS, shouldn't they be taking this guy out, but I'm glad they don't because he's 15 for 15, and I know, I mean I don't really know, but I'm knowing so many things all at once, that this guy's never in his life played like this. JESUS CHRIST, get him out of there, is all I can think, but it's not what I want—and now in my other world, I'm seeing every ICBM installation in every farmer's field in every state of the union, in every country in the world, and Number 8 fades back, he's looking to the sideline, then downfield, and I'm seeing the guy who has the job of turning the key in a kind of control panel. IS THERE A WORD FOR THIS THING THE KEY GOES INTO?— anyway, he's the guy who has to push the button, to let the missiles fly, and at the same time, Number 8 is really going for it, and the other guy is going long, downfield, so Number 8 pumps, and this other guy in my mind is closing his eyes, like he doesn't want to know if the Atlas boosters are really lifting off, he just knows he's got to push this button; he isn't even sure if the missiles he's sending outbound will even get there before he's clobbered with however many megatons they manage to pack into warheads these days, unbearable heat for whatever fraction of a second it takes for a human being to vaporize, and Number 8 pumps again when the pass rusher closes in from the side of the TV, and Number 8 lets the ball fly like a bird from his hand, under its own power, its own ability to seek glory—and just in that moment when it leaves his fingertips, just in that microsecond when I'm crying inside to have my wife come in and see this terrible and beautiful thing, just in that spot in time, Number 8's arms fall to his side. He's actually watching the thing sail up, long, down the field, its spiral for once seemingly unperturbed by anyone or anything. And he's not doing anything else—it's like he's alive inside a body that's dead with its arms hanging down at its side. It's like he's seeing the same things I can see, seeing everything I told you I could see when I realized this Number 8 was operating on pure faith: there is everything in that spiral, that incredible pigskin ship of holy salvation sailing through the sky, AND THEY KILL HIM, I mean THEY LEVEL THE GUY, I mean HE NEVER HAD A CHANCE.

I mean I ASK YOU, IS THIS NORMAL?
CAN'T ANYBODY DO SOMETHING ABOUT THIS?
IS THIS REALLY HOW THEY'RE SUPPOSED TO PLAY THIS GAME?

My wife comes in and it's like she's been gone a million years. Not because I missed her a million-years worth. But because so much has happened.

Hi, I say, but I want to tell her about the Christly game. I'm busting, and then she asks me.

How was the game?

What a stupid question. Don't you see how it ruins everything? Christ.

DANCE OF EIGHTS

L ate in an early summer day Aron's bees moved through the heavy fronds of a monstrous lilac bush. Among the fronds hung clumps of lavender flowers, shaped so like miniature bunches of grapes I wondered if I might bite into their tiny bitter petals for an intimation of sweetness. The flowers and bees surrounded me, and though I had my back to the monstrous bush, I heard the buzz of one bee crescendo in my left ear, and the fading buzz of this same bee—or what I surmised was this same bee—in the same ear, then another buzz rise in my right ear. I felt the awful sameness of each buzz. The whole midsection of my body sank into the deeply veed seat of my white wooden Adirondack chair. I swiped at the bee with my hand.

My brother Aron sat across from me, and I thought he should say something, anything, about Sylvie and his children he left in the City, but he prattled on about his bees, and I saw behind him the uneven tops of his hives piled over themselves in a rather urban, unplanned sprawling heap of near vertical lines, right angles, and tiny roofs of differing heights, all surrounded by Queen Anne's Lace, rising in thin green stalks, and topped with broad, glaring bunches of white flowers; the stalks jiggled in the breeze, and I suddenly felt all that was happening at once: Aron's murmuring, the stalks jostling one another around the hives, the bees sawing at my right ear, then left . . . and something else. I gave up batting at the bees with my hands, and I now felt queerly indolent and afraid: if it were somehow critical that I must rise from the deeply veed seat of the chair, say, if the bees should suddenly gather from all their various sites in the monstrous bush to a location somehow mysteriously prearranged by insect consent, I would never be able to avoid them. I also felt a strange imbalance in my bodily fluids, or bodily vapors insofar as vapors are fluids of a kind. They seemed to rise and fall with evil disproportion inside my midsection.

I imagined with more than a little horror that I might stay forever in such misery in the enormous canyon of the damnable Adirondack chair.

I asked Aron, "Are you sure you won't come back to the City with me?"

But Aron kept on with his lectures, stories, and precious annotations of the bees . . . all bound up in a narrative of fits and starts, and strange associations, like a bundle of misshapen twigs. I was not angry because he ignored my question. He had answered it twice before, *Yes, I'm sure* and *No, I won't come with you.* I was more taken, in fact amazed, that a dying man could rattle on so. . . .

In time, Aron's tack turned from the bees to other matters. He took "for instance" the blue sky above, and at first I had no idea what his instance illustrated, which of course was not his fault—it was mine, since the Queen Anne's Lace and the hives and the buzzing in one ear and in another were more present and arguably more fascinating than Aron's talking about them—but he gave me this unconnected instance of the "blue, blue" cloudless sky above us, "one big thing all around," and then another instance, "a sudden gust of air" funneling between the house and the hives and the monstrous lilac bush, and shooting upward into the birches, then descending from those uppermost branches to "swoop down and around us. . . ."

"And a sky just before dusk dazzles me," he said with his head cocked back looking at the sky. "The corners of the horizon seem turned upward; everything is turned upward, over me, and into a new feeling each time I see such a sky. A gust of wind does the same thing, only different, somehow, I am not sure how."

"So tell me what you feel."

"An ache in my neck, a corresponding ache in the blue sky and the wind."

"Your neck hurts because you've been looking up at the sky so long and talking at the same time."

"No. It's a corresponding ache; the sky aches blue, my neck aches blue."

"I haven't a pain in the neck—other than you."

"Wise ass . . . since I've been sick I feel in bodily masses about things."

"Things?"

"Not history, or the future, or the general present, I mean things that happen when they are happening: I feel them in my body."

"So where do you feel, say, sad?"

"My legs."

"And what is happening when you feel sad in your legs?"

"The bees make oddly shaped eights when they dance on the combs, concentrically with one another—so many edges of each eight touches so many edges of others. I wonder if that touching of edges is ever enough for them to say anything to each other—yet they know; they say things with their little dance, for instance, how close or far the next lilac bush may be from the hive. One bee tells this bee or another to follow it here or there." I batted at a bee that seemed to buzz a bit too loudly and I assumed therefore incautiously close to my right ear. I quickly withdrew my hand from the lilac bush and held it stiffly at my side to avoid a sting. Then Aron added, "You want to know when I'm coming back, but I cannot tell you I am coming back."

I was thinking how this was more like the old Aron I had known when we were growing up. Aron the indecisive, Aron the metaphysical, Aron inconclusive; in a way, thinking back on all his little character flaws helped me climb a few notches out of my indolence. I slid forward and up a fraction of an inch in my chair to show him I was paying him greater attention.

"Do you ever feel anything in your pancreas," I asked him, "or in

and around your pancreas? Didn't Eighteenth-Century scientists believe the soul was located there? Do things happen that cause you to
feel with your pancreas?"

"No, never," he said in an inappropriately serious way. "I never
feel with my pancreas."

Aron jerked his body forward and began to rise from his chair. A
short while the forward momentum of his body worked against grav-
ity, and he remained balanced midway up from the chair. His legs
straddled the seat, bent slightly at the knees; then he suddenly over-
came the pull against him and lunged a short distance forward. I flinched
somewhere in my body because I felt he was coming at me, and I was
too hopelessly far down in my own chair to respond. A moment he
stood over me. He looked tired and ashen in his face—except for an
intimation of pink around his eyes. He wanted, perhaps even needed,
to rest.

"Come on," he said. "Let's go inside."

"No," I said, "I'll have more tea," and I lowered my eyes. He walked
around the back of his chair to the table, poured tea into his glass, then
turned and crossed diagonally to the right of my chair, filled my glass,
set the pitcher back, and crossed on the opposite diagonal to his chair
and sat. It was just so much nonsense, his making the figure of an eight
around our chairs, and since I was sure he did it on purpose, I didn't
mention it. I wouldn't give him the satisfaction. He'd been playing
these games with me all my life, so after a while I tried to keep our
earlier conversation going.

"Where else do you feel things?"

"I'm not sure you are interested," he said, and he cocked his head
back and stared again at the sky, which was now a faint maroon color.

Being so accused, I was suddenly all the more interested. All I
could hope was that Aron sensed I was interested, although I could not
say where in his body he might have sensed it. Moreover, knowing
Aron, I could not *say* I was interested without sounding like, and in-
deed being, a liar. So I hoped he could sense I was interested because I
wanted him to say something about Sylvie and his children.

"I feel things in the back corners of my mouth," he said without changing his gaze from the darkening sky. "I feel angry."

"And what happens to bring this feeling on?"

"That bee—"

He pointed at a bee hovering at my right, near a purple, four-petaled flower in the monstrous lilac bush. I shook my head, and I was certain Aron did not see the little shake, and I turned to watch the bee tickle the inside of the flower with its proboscis, and move back from it.

"What about that bee?"

"It's not the bee, really. It's the awful give and take of things, nectar for pollen, pollen for nectar. Why must everything be exchanged like some absurd tug of war? What's the point? All in all, more is taken than given."

Aron shifted his weight. He drew his buttocks up and came forward in his chair.

"Come on," he said. "Let's go inside."

I did not reply and he sank back heavily into the chair.

I heard him sigh in pain, and I wanted to ask him that moment where and how he felt dying, but I did not. All I could hope was that Aron sensed I wanted to ask him about dying, and would say something about his family so I could get him to come back with me. Then I wondered if there might be inside Aron a place where he could sense I wanted to ask him about dying. I wanted to know if this was the same place he felt dying.

I watched Aron a long while struggling to get up from the Adirondack chair, and I struggled not to help him since I knew he'd only bat me away like one of his bees. The sky grew dark, and drew its dimness over us. I could barely see his face—struggling—then I saw him come out of the chair all at once, as if lifted by an unseen arm from the deep vee, and stand in front of me. I couldn't look at him. I looked away to the bees in the monstrous lilac bush. I watched them. I tried to watch all of them at once moving among the fronds, the clusters of flowers. In the growing dark they looked like shadowy caterpillars crawling among the vague and indecipherable shapes in the bush. They were no longer individuated bees or flowers. I felt the absence of sound.

Aron stood in front of me and he took a deep breath. I hated him when he breathed that way, so deeply, so importantly. It made me feel stupid for being alive. I wanted to know how long he had, how much time they'd given him. I wanted to say to him his sorry soul was in his lungs. I wanted to say he'd better be careful not to hold his breath too long or he'd find out soon where his soul resided when it cried out to breathe. But I didn't say this. . . .

"Will you come with me back to the City?"

"No . . . I want to finish here. I have enough to do here."

I sat awhile with Aron standing in front of me that way.

I couldn't give him the satisfaction of going with him right then— not when he was so obstinate and defiant. He walked away alone and went inside the house. I sensed he knew I would not come with him simply because he wanted me to. When he came back, I got up from my chair and followed him to the hovel of his hives, and the unkempt Queen Anne's Lace. He walked to a short lamppost nearby and put a spotlight on one of the hives. He removed the front of the hive and we watched the bees, the mass of individuated bodies bump and strain to make their eights. I tried to decode the smallest and most oblique patterns from the mass of moving thoraxes, the touching and groping, the quivering antennae. But I couldn't make any sense of it, and I suddenly wanted to tell Aron he was a liar to have claimed he could, a liar to confuse higher truth with an indecipherable system of signs.

"Where do you feel Sylvie—your children—the rest of us?" I asked him.

He was silent, and I looked inside myself for the place to feel the dance of eights, and I could not find the place, or the feeling of the place, or the feeling of Aron or Aron's family anymore.

He shut up the hive and turned off the spotlight. Fireflies gathered in the monstrous lilac, signaling: something light, something dark . . . something given, something taken. . . . Except for the fireflies, the dark was all around me. I was nearly blind. I started forward in the dark and felt the hairs of Aron's arm brush against mine, and I knew from that most intimate and remote sensation that the unnameable thing and its place existed in me, knew my brother would never come with me, knew the unnameable thing and its place would never allow him to come with me. "This way," he said, and he took my arm in his hand and led me back through the hives to the house.

THE CALIFORNIA FRANCHISE
TAX BOARD

My name is Peter Brengel and I have died. My daughter doesn't know. I think she is too excited to notice I am dead. She receives her French horn today.

Before I died, the band director asked me if I wanted to rent the French horn for a two-month trial or to buy it outright. My daughter begged, so I bought it outright. I had to buy the case, too. Six hundred dollars. Now, my daughter waits for the band director to pick her horn up at the music store and drop it by the house.

The French horn will be an *Olds*. Its case will be shaped like a large snail. My daughter says the French horn's case is ugly; but you take the horn from the case and you can see your face in its bell. My daughter says the French horn case won't fit under the bus seat. She says she will need two seats, empty and complete. She's made arrangements with the bus driver and her friends for the extra space.

My daughter says the French horns two other kids have are beautiful. She says hers will be as nice. Including the case. She can't wait to get her French horn; she can't wait to tell me. She doesn't know I am dead.

The people at the California Franchise Tax Board do not know I have died. They are in Sacramento. They have a toll-free number if you have questions or a change of address. If you are concerned about the proper treatment of your income. I am not sure how I should notify them I have died. Technically, being dead, I am a non-resident. Still, I lived in the state of California for part of the taxable year in which I *was*. Which would mean I am a *partial resident*. If I could tell my daughter I am dead, she could ask them if I need to file if I am a *partial-* or *dead-* or *non-*resident. But perhaps this is neither here nor there. Perhaps I am neither here nor there. Technically tax is due and, according to "Publication 540NR," they have ways of getting tax due no matter where you are. This is called garnishment of wages. I prefer *attachment*; there is more compassion in the latter.

My wife understands taxes better than me. Before I died, I told her I did not think we needed to file at all since we were non-residents of California for part of the year in which the tax was due. She disagrees. She reminds me we must file even if we resided in the state for part of the year. Then she exaggerates. *Even one day*, she says.

My wife never misses even one exemption. She tries to squeeze every nickel out of a deduction. Unlike my daughter, who will be getting her French horn today, my wife knows I am dead. But she will not admit it.

My dog knows I am dead. He admits it freely in whatever language he uses to convey this to me. My dog can see me. This very moment I am trying to tell him how I died. He does not understand. He only wants to play in the way a dog wants to play when you don't want to. My dog is always ready to play. Before I died, I always quit our little games first. He scorned me. Dada the *quitter*.

Now I am dead. Now I play with him endlessly. He always quits first. It's payback, you see, for all the long faces he gave me. I am dead. I have lots of time now for my dog, the only one who can see me.

I am trying to tell my dog how I died. He still does not understand. He wants to play. His tongue is long and his eyes are bright. Now he thinks twice about it. He trots off.

My name is Peter Brengel and I have died because I know music, and I do not know taxes. For example, I know French horns do not have spit valves. If I were alive I would tell my daughter this: you need to remove the mouthpiece, set a towel down on the carpet, and rotate the French horn so the spit comes out the bell. My daughter will have to learn about spit valves herself. I am dead. I am glad I can't tell her about draining the spit because it's kind of sickening.

I played the trombone as a youth. Less tubing. And it has a spit valve. It's easier to drain than the French horn and less expensive. The French horn cost six hundred dollars outright. But I love the hearty noble sound of the French horn over the trombone. The sound is richer. It's probably worth the extra money. It will take my daughter years to make the sound the way I know it should be. It would have been worth the wait. I love my daughter. My daughter can't know this. I am dead. I hope she will get private lessons. It puts you ahead of other kids. It matters through high school anyway.

We rented. I taught music. That is how I know French horns do not have spit valves. I didn't think I earned a lot teaching music. Perhaps I did. I was learning fast about taxes before I died. Form 540NR is for non-residents. "NR" for non-resident. "540," who knows. Tax is due based on earnings while a resident of California as a proportion of whole earnings for the taxable year . . . as reported on line 33 of the Federal Return, less special California credits, exemptions, and deductions. California has a Renters' Credit. . . . But will I owe the California Franchise Tax Board six hundred dollars if I am dead?

My daughter comes in with her new French horn. My wife is on the carpet with a coffee and the 540NR. My dog is exhausted from playing with me. He has made a cocoon by my wife on the carpet.

My daughter announces she needs to study her whole notes. She needs to blow a *C*. A good *C* before tomorrow.

I tell her there's nothing like a good *C*. I tell her do not disturb your mother. Or the dog. They are mad at me. I tell her it is tax time. I tell her I should have withheld more. I owe the California Franchise

Tax Board six hundred dollars. I tell her I am dead now. She tells me I am not. We laugh.

WHAT ROUGH BEASTS

Two of them milled about the trolley stop on T. Vrublevskio Street by the Great Cathedral in Vilnius. The other eight were in the trees nearby. Perhaps the two at the stop pretended to mill. They were not like dogs in the old days. They stopped milling. Waited. Started again. They had a plan. . . .

One was small and white with stub legs, and his eyes were pink, shot through with blood. He was sniffing the base of the metal pole upon which the trolley schedule was fastened—and above that the bus schedule. He kept sniffing like that and pissed the pole twice. His eyes rolled upward, glanced at the trolley schedule. The other was bigger, long legs, and black with yellowish eyes and bristling hair. He paced between the trunks of two oaks, head down, eyes slightly lifted as if he expected something to suddenly drop from the branches. Both were thin. Ribs showing. Plenty of garbage was strewn about the trolley stop, but neither of them seemed interested in eating it. The disinterest was in their eyes.

Stubs suddenly paddled across the street and sat at the feet of a woman who stood beneath an extension ladder propped against the side of a building. Just left of the ladder was an archway under which peddlers sold political books in many languages from flimsy card tables. The woman stood beneath the ladder as if waiting for someone to come down it. But no one was on the ladder. And no one came down. Soon,

Stubs seemed to grow bored waiting with the woman and recrossed the street to the trolley stop, which brought Long Legs out to the curb, where both dogs rubbed snouts, then resumed their vigils at the stop. Stubs sniffed his pole again and pissed it—one of those half-squirts where the gesture exceeds the substance of the piss itself—then yawned.

When a trolley came it was the Five. It was a yellow trolley with red trim, all its color the result of paint put on directly over large patches of rust that stood in splotches along its sides. The trolley car whined and rattled as it made the turn off Gedimino Prospect and left onto T. Vrublevskio. While the trolley completed its turn, torsos of passengers all together slanted right, then popped back to center. The spring-loaded contacts on the wires above the street twanged and a few blue sparks flew. The old yellow box slowed and stopped. Stubs and Long Legs ran to the curb to meet the trolley, from which only two people emerged, a boy with a fishing pole and an old woman with a large jar of currants poking out her purse. Long Legs went back to prowl between the two oaks. Stubs stayed awhile longer at the curb.

When the door slapped shut and the Five whined away from the stop, the wind came up suddenly, raising Stubs' ears, and he went back to his pole, sniffing and pissing it. The wind atomized the droplets of piss, and a pale yellow mist flew about the feet of a man reading his newspaper. There was so much spray one had to wonder where a dog obtained such quantities of fluid!

Soon the wind blew even more stiffly. Skirts of women waiting at the stop flew up. They nervously tucked their purses into the pits of their arms and used their free hands to press their hems to their knees. Men held their hats or covered their eyes. People ran for the insides of the Great Cathedral. Leaves were tumbling everywhere. Long Legs and Stubs did not alter their routines. Only Long Legs hesitated—yawned—then pushed on, trotting between the two oak trunks.

Across the street at a kavinė a gigantic white umbrella lifted off from one of the sidewalk tables; it flew up, over the street in a startling arc, so high so suddenly that Stubs reared up on his two back legs. Long Legs stopped pacing and put his ears up. Four men came racing out the kavinė and cocked their heads back to spot the fugitive umbrella, which had made its way an astonishing distance to the clock affixed to the bell tower of the Great Cathedral, where it crashed into the Roman numeral IX on the face of the clock and slid down the plaster surface of the tower to a group of young people huddled below with all sorts of rings and jewels adorning their epidermises, hair and faces painted, all colors. The four men from the kavinė rushed into the street and were nearly struck by a police car, its siren blaring, horn blasting in strange harmony with the siren. The four men seemed to dance, skipping gracefully out of the police car's way, and in one quick movement continued their dash for the bell tower and the fallen umbrella, which by now had scuttled its way across the piazza of the Great Cathedral and lodged itself against one of the huge white columns of the main entrance. One of the men reached the umbrella first—but he had no sooner taken it by its pole, when one of its ribs swung out, the flap of fabric fastened to the rib caught a new gust of wind, and it flew into the fatherly arms of Moses' statue in the portico—a rather larger than life rendering, four times larger to be exact—at which time the first man was joined by the other three and they caught the umbrella. Two of the men gathered the umbrella's fabric in and folded its ribs tightly against the pole, then all four took hold of the fabric, ribs and pole with one fist each, and began to march it—against the wind— back across the piazza toward the street and the kavinė. They had scarcely reached the bell tower when the umbrella suddenly exploded open, its ribs inverted—lugging them backwards with the wind. Then the wind suddenly died and the umbrella snapped shut, trapping all four men inside against the center pole!

Stubs and Long Legs paced, waited, all the while the wind carried things away, while people went about pinning things down and retrieving them from distant places. The men trapped inside the umbrella eventually got it open and, exhausted, escorted the errant umbrella back to its kavinė, where they carefully threaded it through the hole in the white plastic table, and replaced the chairs carefully to four equilateral positions around it.

When another trolley arrived, the Seven, both Stubs and Long Legs
dashed into the trees and benches in the small park behind the stop.
Just as the Seven was loading, they both re-emerged from the trees
with a third dog, a small reddish collie-like mongrel. Red trotted up to
the lower metal step of the trolley and pissed it, just as a woman with
two pails of potatoes took the stairs into the trolley. A bit of the piss
caught the stocking of her panty hose and she started to scream, but the
trolley doors slammed, trapping her inside; it jolted ahead, and one
could only see the screaming expression on her face through the window.

Red joined Stubs and Long Legs. Red sniffed Stubs' ass; then Stubs
sniffed Red's ass; then Stubs and Red both sniffed Long Leg's ass—
twice each—after which Long Legs returned to his sentry duty at the
oaks. Stubs ran into the trees of the small park, and Red took his place
sniffing and pissing the pole below which the trolley schedule was
posted. Three more trolley cars came and left. But no dog boarded
them.

Soon, the day grew shorter, night came on, and a beggar arrived at
the trolley stop. He made that grand entrance beggars sometimes make,
staggering in, wearing a Red Army coat with ghost patches in the coarse
dirty green fabric, where insignias of all shapes and sizes were torn
away. But the real grandeur he displayed in occasioning the trolley
stop was in his hands. He had none—and where his hands had been
there were two stumps. Leather purses were sewn directly into the
flesh of the two stumps. Two more purses were sewn onto the fabric of
his trousers at his knees. As the beggar made his way through the people
at the stop, he swung his hand-purses to and fro, this way, that, like
two great pauperish pendulums, cutting a great swath of pity among
the people as he moved though them, some who even stuck out the
sides of their very own hands to momentarily stop the momentous
momentum of the beggar's hand-purses to quickly untie the flap on the
purse and drop coins inside. His debut completed, the beggar stag-
gered to the base of one of Long Legs' oaks and, extending his arms
before him for balance, ceremoniously slid, back to tree, downward,

until he rested, his knees pointing at Heaven, arms upon those two great promontories, purse-stumps extended ever outward, revealing yet a fifth purse, seemingly sewn into the pit of his right arm, close to his ribs.

Red yawned, made a backward glance at the beggar, and pissed the pole. Long Legs stopped pacing at the opposite oak, sat, and stared vacantly at the beggar, who, having no idea what the vacant stare of the dog could mean, kindly entreated Long Legs to join him.

"Dog!" he called. "Here, good dog!"

He continued to fling these endearments at Long Legs until Red came by and, tolerating but one pat of the beggar's purse-stumps at his brow, pissed the beggar's trousers at one knee, turned, and went back to the pole with the trolley schedule.

The beggar rose and left the trolley stop. More people left. The day grew small. Smaller. But Red and Long Legs remained. Another trolley came, the Eight, but neither dog budged. Then, just at dusk, a special air show began—three vintage World War II fighters buzzed the city in swooping, frightening formations. The pounding of pistons echoed against the façades of old buildings that had survived the war years, concussive sounds that rattled through alleys and medieval court-yards. Red put his head back and followed the show. Long Legs paced between the two oaks, his ears back, muscles in them twitching time to time as they followed the war sounds overhead. After a short time the city trembled once more and the war birds sped under the Kalvariŭ bridge over the Neris River and disappeared in the west over the foot-bridge a little downstream. Red and Long Legs stood dog-still at the curb in the dimming light. They were hatching a plan. Something grand. Something unthinkable.

More trolleys came and went. Darkness came on. More people wandered away from the stop. Some grabbed taxis from the stand on the street near the bell tower. Others went off toward the river for long walks home. Little by little, all the people drifted away from the trol-ley stop, until none remained, until deep in the night the Seventeen came, another old job, whining around the bend off Gedimino Prospect, yellow inside with old light, its blue sparks licking lines overhead. Its doors popped out. Red and Long Legs dashed for the doors. And others, Stubs in the lead, seven more in all, dashed out the trees for the Seventeen.

At the deserted trolley stop on T. Vrublevskio, the Seventeen carries ten dogs, just ten, and its driver. When the Seventeen pulls away, seven dogs sit in seats facing the curbside. They sit eerily erect; their tongues loll out; their gazes remain straight ahead. As the trolley pulls ever farther away, three others sit on the long bench seat in the rear window. Long Legs. Stubs. Red. They stare vacantly outward from the old yellow light inside. Unlike the other seven dogs, these three gaze straight behind; but like the other dogs on the trolley, like all the dogs of Vilnius, one cannot know from their steadfast stares why they have undertaken this trip, or what they intend on their journey, or what it is these rough beasts will do when they arrive.

OVERTURES

I meant to say something about what happened after I discovered a miserable pile of stones twenty-five kilometers north of Vilnius. The stones mark the geographical center of Europe, a place not on my maps, though if you get around as much as I do you'll find places like that. . . . After departing this pile of stones, I took the bus back to Vilnius via the Molėtai Highway, stopped at my flat on the Neris River, and intended to ring you up. I wanted to skip that pile of stones, tell you all about Wagner's *Overture to the Flying Dutchman*, and ask you to come out with me to hear it. But when I got to my flat I was famished, and made myself all the hungrier watching from my window the crests of ashes and birches along the Neris River quivering in an easterly breeze, purple, red, orange, tannic tones fluting the bottom edge of a cloudless autumn sky. . . .

I soon found myself standing in the doorway of the vast and largely occupied Valgykla "Tulip," what had been the cooperative's cafeteria in Soviet times. I didn't want to be alone, though among so many diners I felt overwhelmed. I leaned a little right on the doorjamb and surveyed the room. Only two people sat by themselves, the first a man who seemed peaceful, waiting to be served. I envied him, then realized he must be lonely. A single strand of ratted hair hung in his eyes. It must have reminded him of his loneliness; every now and again he rolled his eyes up, saw the shadow cast by that ratted hair, seemed to sigh, and I almost left straightaway to ring you and go out to hear the *Dutchman*—when suddenly a battalion of servers, all dressed in white, began to sweep through the aisles; so I moved a little forward to get a look at what they were putting out for people, a roast of beef with vegetables and fruit pounded and baked inside: garlic cloves, carrots, onions, and prunes. My favorite.

I became especially intrigued when at the far side of the Tulip I saw a pair of women, one speaking, the other listening. . . . I crossed the room, going right, by way of the aisle formed by the tables and wall, nudging a chair now and again carefully, quietly, steering as close to the wall as possible without drawing attention to myself by staying too close to it. For a time I stood in another doorjamb at the side entrance of the Tulip, watching this pair of women, their eyes intent on one another's faces, some unseen hand seeming to hold back the ritual clanking of knives and forks and permitting them perfect conversation! The speaker's dark eyes slightly lifted as she spoke, words in her mouth framed by short raven-black hair; every so often she'd tap the side of her plate with the tip of a finger to punctuate a phrase. I realized then that it might be possible for me to listen in on their conversation and go unnoticed.

I went straight to their table, quietly placed my napkin on my lap, and waited for the server to come. I closed my eyes, waiting for one or both of these women to suddenly react to my presence . . . but they didn't. I even leaned a little forward to test the two women, to see how completely they were engaged with one another; then I let a little air out of my chest, softly.

The server came with my food, slid my plate in front of me, and I almost flinched hearing the slight sound of its bottom rubbing the tablecloth. I put my eyes down, as if putting them down would erase the sound of the plate rubbing the cloth. I held my breath, then lifted one eye slightly and saw them still speaking. I gingerly lifted my fork and knife—both at precisely the same time—why use two actions when one would do?—then realized, all the time hearing the speaker's voice steady and unperturbed, that I was even hungrier than before, and for meat, glorious meat and not the usual grayish cabbage and potatoes, and even dared to stab ever so cautiously into the meat with my fork, raise the knife slightly, then bring it down on the roast and begin to delicately saw, using only the pressure derived from the weight of the knife itself to cut my fruit-filled meat. Then and only then did I ever so surreptitiously turn my full attention to the teller and her story. . . .

This happened when my mother was a child, in Vilnius, during the war. I don't really know how old my mother was in those days. You never get that sort of thing out of some parents. How many people really know their parents? I mean, where they came from, what they cared about, all about things they did or felt when they were young and alone. All my mother said was that she was a child and she was an only child. I mean, there was a woman hidden in my mother's flat, or so my mother believed because her parents had told her this woman was there, standing behind a wall, with scarcely enough room to sit when she needed to sleep. My mother's parents said to her, 'Don't worry about her. You must not ever tell anyone that this woman is in the wall. If you see her, you must never speak to her. If you do, something terrible will happen to all of us.'

My mother did not know in which wall or where in a particular wall this woman was hiding. She imagined the woman stood behind the wall with her ear to a water pipe so she could hear all the sounds in the building, then when the flat fell silent she'd come out, use the toilet, eat a little, then go back into hiding.

Everyone knows the stories of those days. . . . My mother's parents both worked, times were tough, and so my mother was left alone in the flat during the day. The landlady lived in the building, too, and she told my mother's parents, 'Don't worry, I can check on the child from time to time.'

Well, of course, knowing a woman was concealed in their wall, my mother's parents were reluctant to allow this. But how could they not in those days? The Nazi occupation. So my mother's parents told the landlady that she could come up once a day in the late morning to check on my mother.

Things were normal at first. The landlady would come to the flat at the appointed hour. She was a portly lady who enjoyed fatty foods very much, was of course fat herself from enjoying them, and my mother told me that was fortunate for the woman in the wall because my mother imagined the woman could hear the landlady enter the flat, in fact could hear her coming long before she arrived, her thunderous footfalls, distinguishable from any other noise in the building. And because the landlady was so fond of fatty foods she'd bring with her cepelinai and fried pork cutlets, which anyone could easily smell from a great distance, and which she shared with my mother. She'd make a little tea and the two of them would have an early dinner.

Soon after the landlady came to watch my mother, she said, 'Come, child, let me show you how to make your parents' bed.'

The landlady had obviously determined that the bed regularly went unmade since my mother's parents went off to their jobs quite early; and so she took my mother by the hand into the bedroom, where the blankets on the bed were tossed-up and resembled a pachyderm. Attracted by such an odd shape, my mother began to approach the bed, when suddenly the landlady shoved her from behind with such force that she sailed over the footboard into the center of the bed and crushed the tossed-up pachyderm, flat. Instantly, my mother thought, 'I've crushed a pachyderm—how?'

The landlady, who could not have known that the tossed-up shape in the bed was that of a pachyderm, said, 'You've flung yourself into your parents' bed! Why? Is someone hiding in those sheets?'

What I really wanted to tell you about was the story of how I left the Tulip and went out to the university to hear Wagner's *Dutchman*. But it was that landlady's push that drove me past the rest of the story of the woman in the wall and onto the Two trolley going down Antakalnio. When I boarded the trolley I gave my seat to an old man who walked with a cane. The next stop, another elderly man got on and stood in front of me in the aisle. The old man with the cane suddenly reached out with his cane and slashed the elderly man on the calf. The older man turned back to look at me, thinking I'd struck him, then saw the crippled man with the cane sitting and, after a long time shouting at him rapidly in Lithuanian, produced an umbrella, lunged past me, began to jab the crippled man in his stomach, who immediately repelled the attack by parrying with his cane, after which the man with the umbrella quickly refined his technique and started to thrust—and parry—when the man with the cane did the same. I'd often wondered how I'd react to something like this. I let it happen. I almost laughed watching the two men locked in swordplay! A woman with a basket of peas finally stopped the fray, batting the cane and umbrella away with her hands, saying to both men—and me— "Has sanity vanished from the face of the Earth? You shame yourselves and the rest of us!"

After I got off the trolley, I walked to Vokiečių gatvė to find a phone booth to call you. Somehow I felt drawn to you given your description by our mutual friend, Erika, who'd given me your telephone number and assured me she'd put me in good stead. Has Erika spoken to you? No matter. Somehow, though you hardly knew me, I thought you might save my day, say, perhaps, "But you mustn't blame yourself for those two old men fighting. It is more common than you think. Perhaps they were enemies from long ago, in the ice age, Soviet times."

When I'd decided to ring you up, I wanted to be alone. And there was no one in the plaza of Vokiečių, something someone especially notices when they want to be left alone, like a bitter little miracle. The sky was vacant and blue, no wind whatsoever. The butt of the receiver felt heavy in my palm, nothing else, a single sensation. When you answered my call, I said, laughing, "Erika gave me your number. I have two tickets for the *Flying Dutchman*. . . . Don't stand me up."

You replied quickly, "Let me go."

"Do you mean," I replied slowly, "'let me go' as in 'I need to get

off the telephone now' or 'Let me go' as in 'Let me go—forever'?"
But there was a rattling silence on the line, so I quickly added, "I'm
harmless, believe me. . . . All right, forget about my asking you to go
with me to the *Flying Dutchman*. What I really want now is to tell
you about a strange occurrence on the Two trolley—a fight! At least
let me explain."

"Let me go," you said again.

"But why be so dramatic?" I replied. "I'm closer than you think!
I'm just at the telephone booth on Vokiečių. Don't stand me up!" I
insisted.

"Let me go," you said.

My mother never told her parents about the landlady's shoving her
into their bedclothes. You know how a child feels ashamed about
things, any little thing sometimes, the way the innocent sometimes
bear evil away with them. So the landlady kept visiting my mother in
the flat with the woman hidden in the wall. One day, she said to my
mother, 'Now we are going to play a game.' Then she tugged my
mother by her arm outside the flat and into the hallway. 'Stand here,'
the landlady added, then walked to the doors of three flats on that
floor, and with her master key unlocked them. The landlady left each
door swinging free, slightly ajar. When she finished unlocking the
doors to the three other flats she returned to my mother. 'I want you
to hide in one of those three flats and I'll come and try to find you.
I'll close my eyes now. You have only three minutes to hide—now,
go!'

The landlady covered her eyes and my mother darted off and ran
in and out of the first flat, and when she went into the second flat and
ran into the bedroom, she saw a woman draped in a long black shawl
coming out of the closet! The woman started toward my mother, who
backed away in surprise.

'Don't be afraid,' the woman said sweetly to my mother. Then
the woman smiled, or as mother recalls it, tried to smile, the way the
spirit smiles but the face resists and will not permit the muscles to

move freely. The woman held her hand out to my mother, who, astonished that there could be two women hiding in the walls of two flats of the building, turned and raced out of the flat and into the hallway, hearing behind only a remnant of the woman's final words, 'Please.'

To my mother's surprise the landlady was not in the hall or searching any of the flats whose doors she'd so ceremoniously opened. Instead, my mother could hear the landlady's thunderous footfalls in her parents' flat, and when she went inside the landlady was rounding the corner, coming out of my mother's bedroom.

'I thought I told you to hide in one of the other flats,' the landlady said.

My mother had felt ashamed when the landlady had pushed her into the tossed-up bedclothes; and now she felt ashamed having met the woman coming out of the closet, and so she lied about having seen her. 'You are looking in the wrong place!' my mother said to the landlady, nearly in tears. 'You will never find me in here!'

Please understand: though I scarcely knew you, I'd hated letting you go, hanging up that receiver and pushing off for the university alone. But when I found the iron gate of the courtyard of Saint Jonas's Cathedral at the university, what a splendid sight greeted me! *At last!* I thought. *Hohoje! Hohoje! Halloho! Ho!*—through the iron bars I could see the city orchestra, all its members in tuxedos and tails, feverishly playing the *Flying Dutchman*. In the full and clear light of the evening sun, their trembling instruments made slender, crisp, exquisite shadows that vibrated on the cobblestones. I entered the courtyard, at last full of hope and anticipation after what had been a day of setbacks, ready to drink the music until I'd become intoxicated and unafraid. Yet just as I passed through the iron gate the *Dutchman's* last note sounded—an eerie reflection off the medieval walls of the courtyard. So near my long-awaited goal, Fate had reserved the last blow! The audience applauded, musicians began to pack away their instruments. I could do nothing but stand there the whole time, until the last soul in the courtyard, a cellist, walked past me at the iron gate, his cello case wobbling in front of him. He looked like a pregnant woman. I almost laughed. In my bad Lithuanian I said to him, "I only heard your last note!"

The cellist laughed and stared at me, but not straight at me; he looked past me to a point on the ancient and fractured wall of the courtyard where that last note of the *Dutchman* had resounded. And when the cellist went through the iron gate, I was alone, and in that condition was reminded that this cellist's stare was perhaps what I'd wanted all along, why I'd wanted to hear the *Dutchman* in the first place, a little game I like to play: I sit close to the musicians; make eye contact with one of them; try to toss the musician off a beat or two; but the best I can do is to get a musician to stare in my general direction, beyond me—while the music, unperturbed, rises around me, drowns my senses, and I've no choice but to listen and listen while the musician's grim gaze goes past me, back to that same spot on the same wall again and again and again. . . .

After the game of searching the three flats on my mother's floor, the landlady did not come around for two days. But the next time she came to check on my mother, she entered very quietly, no thunderous footfalls; she was grinning ear to ear, seemed very self-satisfied, grinned so long my mother could not help but grin herself. The landlady pointed to the sitting room.

'Let's go in there,' the landlady whispered. 'We're going to play another game.' She sat on the couch and removed some cookies from a paper bag. She handed one to my mother, who eagerly ate it. 'Here,' she went on, and withdrew a handkerchief from her purse. The handkerchief was bright white and thoroughly perfumed. The scent nearly made my mother faint, but remembering the cookies, my mother put her back straight and listened as the landlady continued, 'I'll tie this over your eyes. Then I am going to place your hand in some things. I want you to tell me what these things feel like. If you are correct, I will give you another cookie.'

'All right!' my mother replied, and the landlady tied the perfumed handkerchief over her eyes.

First, the landlady took my mother by her hand, guided her to a potted plant, and pushed her fingers into the soil.

'Earth,' my mother said, snuffling from the perfume in the handkerchief.

'Correct,' the landlady replied, 'and here's your cookie.'

Next, the landlady walked my blindfolded mother to a small bowl with water inside.

'Water,' she replied and received her cookie.

Next, the landlady lit a candle and held my mother's hand a few centimeters above the flame.

'Fire,' my mother whispered, full of breath, wonder and a little anger. She wrenched her hand from the landlady's cold, fat fingers, and tore the blindfold from her eyes.

'I didn't hear you,' the landlady whispered. Then she said, loudly, 'What? What is it!'

'Fire!' my mother said, loudly as well, and angrier still. 'I told you! Fire!'

The storyteller lowered her eyes; her gaze fell to the table; her face grew dark and she looked at her hands then looked back to her devoted listener. 'Well,' the storyteller said, and she paused.

I wondered: what heat, what fear or courage could have caused this woman to stay inside her wall when the shouts of this child spelled almost certain death?

My mouth was open. I knew it. My tongue was dry. I set my knife and fork aside, and all the air seemed to rush out of me. Suddenly the storyteller's eyes darted right—to me—then to my plate—she seemed astonished that I had seated myself, been served, and begun to eat, all in the time she'd told her story and that she'd not noticed any of it. She discovered me! She smiled grimly, forming a flat line with her lips, turned ever so slightly at the corners. All I could think was that this was not what I had started out to do. I was off to attend a concert,

Wagner's *Dutchman*. And I was going to tell you about that, only that, and now this? I couldn't help myself. I waited a very short while for her grim smile to change, but her every feature seemed frozen.

"What do you mean 'Well'?" I said to her. "Did she come out of that wall or not?" I paused, trying to gain my composure, but no luck. "How could she!" I said angrily. I looked at her coldly—and I flew. I left my food—I left everything. . . .

All this is a long way around telling you I understand why you won't come out with me. I understand your horror as clearly as I understand my own. It goes all the way back to the woman in the wall, whether one allows cruelty to hold sway in the world or not—or to travel, by which I mean I encountered the strangest man today. . . . After hearing the last note of the *Dutchman* come off the wall of the courtyard of Saint Jonas's at the university, I headed back to Vokiečių to ring you again, which I did, but got no answer, and soon found myself sitting on the steps of the Vilnius Museum of Art, swinging my legs over the wall supporting the steps, my back to the museum, which by that time of day was closed, locked tight. I liked feeling the weight of the concrete building looming behind me. No surprises.

In the street, there was a taxi, an old gray Moskvich, motor running, the driver sitting on the hood, smoking, swinging his legs back and forth. I began to synchronize the swinging of my legs with his, back, forth; but when I was sure I'd found the point at which our two sets of swinging legs were synchronized, the taxi driver abruptly changed his rhythm and threw me out of synch. So caught up in my little game with the taxi driver, swinging our legs like that, the old man seemed to come out of nowhere, suddenly sailing slowly up the steps of the museum toward me. By now, the sun was low in the western sky, so his shadow preceded him. His eyes were wide and shot through, blood-red, and with a white handkerchief he was wiping sweat dappling his forehead. He stopped one step below mine, his back leg on the step before that one. He looked up at me.

"American?" he said, out of breath.

"Yes," I said. (How'd he know, I've asked myself a thousand times. Was I really so transparent?)

"I am retired, you know," he went on. "I am French." He folded his handkerchief, reached back, and pushed it into his hip pocket. "I am a professor of history, you know. This place is so full of history."

"Standing room only," I said. "Center of Europe."

He nodded at the Art Museum behind us. "Closed?" he said.

"Closed," I said.

"Time to find another?"

"No."

"Are you sure?"

"It's too late," I said. "Everything's closed and I'm moving on. Next thing, I'm grabbing that taxi over there."

He looked a little puzzled at my remark, then shrugged and looked all around himself, skyward, sighing, tired. For a moment I thought about telling him the story of the woman in the wall. But then the lids of his eyes suddenly fell and I thought he might expire on the steps. All I could think is that I couldn't have him dropping there in front of me. Not after all I'd been through.

"By the way," he said at last, "the geographical center of Europe. Have you found it?"

"No," I said.

"It's a pity," he said.

"No, it isn't," I replied. "Get away from me," I added. "Leave me alone."

WOMAN WITHOUT ARMS

He sat in a chair at the window and considered the woman, the poet, who sat on one side of the bed across the room. The woman had been without arms since birth, since time immemorial as she had once told him, and the universal joints at her shoulders and elbows were metal and blue. Her prostheses were smooth and plaster-colored, attached at her shoulders with a thick plastic brace. Shiny hooks and pincer devices, loaded with springs and stay nuts, were fixed at the ends of her artificial limbs.

He watched her use the tip of one hook to prod a tiny edge of foil jutting from a small banana-yellow pack of chewing gum. She rolled one shoulder back, jerked her torso slightly, and the flat silver stick of gum slid from the pack. She carefully transferred the stick to the other hook, and used her free hook to turn over the minute sawtooth jag of foil along the seam, then she ran the hook under and along the seam until she provoked the whole wrapper from the stick of gum. She craned her neck over the hook and took the bare stick between her teeth. She rolled the stick into her mouth with her tongue. She chewed the gum voraciously, breathing through her nose.

He watched her perform such minute tasks with fascination, yet his feelings about the woman went deeper than fancy. Now, having her in the hotel with him, and in the eventide light, he saw how she was composed, how these things and ideas of these things ordered themselves in his eyes, behind his eyes, deeper in his mind. The pupils in her eyes were a color of steel, but oddly racy and blue in weaker light. Her skin was the color of milk, and when she crossed her legs under her light cotton gown, she exposed a sliver of skin under the parabolic veil of her gown. Her hair was blonde, limp, and glossy; much of the time a swatch of the limp hair swung half-over her face; she never moved the patch of hair aside since she hadn't the hands for it; nor did she shake it away with her head; she seemed to accept its soft shade, and he accepted the shade and the memory of the things around her, things that became her, and became memory in the shade of his mind. She was shapely regardless of attire, and he remembered the stealth of her body without her prostheses, the sleek, soft curved feeling of her in his hands, the momentum of her body in his hands, her unusually wonderful balance, the warm sense of centeredness he felt when he held her close to him.

She was chewing the gum and he knew she'd chewed the sugar out of it because she slowed her chewing and spoke.

"So, you think you know how it feels," she said, and turned in the bed, away from him, to face the wall.

An orange light came down through the part in the curtains near him, bent over the sill, and clove the gray of the room. Outside the hotel he heard the automobile engines sawing and circling the square, splitting from their short-lived confluences around the square into streams down side streets, then the mechanical squeak and clunk of shopkeepers closing up, pushing doors in, testing them to be sure they were secure.

He thought about speaking to the woman, but he could not forget the metal in her skin, the skin in her metal, the blue in her eyes, and the blue in her metal. He made a word in his mind and thought about speaking it, about breaking the tiniest seed of sound in his mind open and letting the word loose in the room, but the word broke off into two parts that were unintelligible, and he held both parts that moment in his mind and knew both parts were from the same word but could not be spoken.

The woman, the poet, slept on her side facing the wall next to the bed, and he lay in the bed, close, behind her. He moved his hands up and down her back, under her gown, until he knew she was aware of him there. He removed her gown and slowly undid the buckles holding her prosthetic brace to her shoulders. He set the brace on the floor beside the bed, slipped off her panties, wrapped his arms around her torso, slipped his penis into her, and made love to her. He closed his eyes to keep from seeing his own hands, his knuckles, his fingernails, clutching the back of her torso, straight in front of him, something that had always been so shocking to him, like watching another man— another man's hands—make love to her, while he was invisible, help- less—or sometimes it was like watching two one-armed men with her, front and back. He felt his muscles flatten and buckle as he came. He noticed how her skin where her arms may have been was smooth, unscarred, not misshapen or perturbed in any way. He heard her . . . was it a sigh?—or something different? Had the simple turning of his head to the right—and his soft barbaric growl—been so selfish? He had put his penis inside her so perfectly, so easily, she had been ready for him—so he thought—and had rolled it about in an enunciation of something: he imagined each wide, circling oscillation of his penis might have left a word broken off inside her, left a word to find its way deep in her, an utterance, a bit of unctuous, yet important noise. Could he have touched her inside with his bit of word?

He fastened the brace onto her shoulders and over her chest. She had not asked him to do it. He was amazed he had taken it up from the floor and done it. But the woman, the poet, did not seem surprised.

He dozed and woke several times. The first time he woke, he saw the woman out of bed, sitting and working at the table by the window. He was sleepy, and he first saw only the woman in the window and the moon in the window. Then he thought in the fog of his mind how the word *working* so pertained to her. He watched her entire torso shake in her chair, her muscles shivering to make the necessary action—the minute quivering—at the tip of her hook where the pen was fastened in it—to form words on the paper. He dozed, and dreamed he saw the words she had written, their delicate shapes on the paper, but he could not understand the words as he dreamt them. He woke later to see the woman standing at the window. Her hooks were cast deep blue in the moonlight, and he wondered how in the world he might keep things just as they were that moment—the blue in the moon, the moon in her blue metal, the metal in her perfect skin, the words the metal in her perfect skin had formed in his dream.

He felt her behind him in the bed at his side, her prostheses—their steel cold—on his hips and over his pelvis. He felt her chin sink lightly into his back. He was looking at his arms, at his hands, and he stared a long while at the black space of the room where he imagined his arms to be; he moved his fingers in his hands, and he believed his fingers were not in his hands, and his arms were not in his shoulders; he moved his fingers and his arms in the empty dark air, and he wanted to believe the loss of his fingers and arms because of the darkness in the room, and the darkness in his mind, and the blue in the moon in his mind, and the moon in her skin in his mind, and the skin in her metal; he could feel her behind him; he could feel the woman, the poet, put her tongue into his ear, her tongue into his mind, her skin into his mind, her metal into his thoughts.

"So you know how it feels," she said, and he felt the words, the tongue deep inside him, the metal in his mind, the touch in her words, and said, "Yes."

Wendell Mayo was born in Corpus Christi, Texas, in 1953. He completed his B.S. in Chemical Engineering at Ohio State University; B.A. in Print Journalism at the University of Toledo; M.F.A. in Fiction at Vermont College; and his Ph.D. in Twentieth-Century Literature at Ohio University. He directs the Creative Writing Program at Bowling Green State University, where he teaches fiction writing, form and theory of fiction, and modern and contemporary literature. He is author of two other books. The first is a story collection, *Centaur of the North* (Arte Público Press), which was the 1997 winner of the Aztlán Prize, and a finalist in both the Violet Crown Book Awards and The Associated Writing Program's Award Series in Short Fiction. The second is a novel-in-stories titled *In Lithuanian Wood* (White Pine Press, 1999). His short stories have appeared widely in over seventy magazines and anthologies, including *The Yale Review, Harvard Review, Missouri Review,* and *Prairie Schooner.* He has been awarded lectureships seven times by the Ministry of Education of the former Soviet Republic of Lithuania. His awards include a Master Fellowship from the Indiana Arts Commission; the HarperCollins Fellowship; resident writer appointments at the MacDowell, Djerassi Foundation, Yaddo, the Edward F. Albee Foundation, and Millay Colony for the Arts; the Eyster Prize; and First Prize in the Mississippi Valley Review Fiction Competition. He is Editor in Chief of the *Mid-American Review.*

Photo: Amy Stillion